GIRL
WHO
STEPPED
INTO THE
PAST

SOPHIE
BARNES

THE GIRL WHO STEPPED INTO THE PAST

Copyright © 2018 by Sophie Barnes

Cover Design and Interior Format

© KILLION
GROUP INC.

BY SOPHIE BARNES

Novels
Christmas at Thorncliff Manor
A Most Unlikely Duke
His Scandalous Kiss
The Earl's Complete Surrender
Lady Sarah's Sinful Desires
The Danger in Tempting an Earl
The Scandal in Kissing an Heir
The Trouble with Being a Duke
The Secret Life of Lady Lucinda
There's Something About Lady Mary
Lady Alexandra's Excellent Adventure
How Miss Rutherford Got Her Groove Back

Novellas
The Duke Who Came To Town
The Earl Who Loved Her
The Governess Who Captured His Heart
Mistletoe Magic (from Five Golden Rings: A
Christmas Collection)

CHAPTER ONE

PUSHING HER RED SPINNER SUITCASE across the platform of King's Cross station, Jane Edwards approached the train that would take her from London to Cloverfield. The Virgin super voyager was more sleek in appearance than the Amtrack she was accustomed to seeing back home in America, which probably meant it was faster too.

Excitement buzzed through her as she boarded one of the carriages and entered the first compartment to her right. After stowing her luggage in the allocated space behind the first row of seats, she paused for a second to glance around. It was mostly empty, allowing her to choose a vacant spot by one of the windows. Hoping to dissuade anyone else from joining her, she placed her bag on the empty seat beside her before settling in for the three hour journey ahead. This was what she wanted, she reminded herself for what had to be the millionth time. Ever since saying goodbye to Geoffrey and leaving New York behind.

Briefly, she admired the arched glass ceiling extending across the platforms. Overall, her impression of England was good so far. The station was neat and orderly, in contrast to the filthy New York subway she was accustomed to. She'd even seen a sign marking Platform ¾, which she wished she'd had time to take a picture next to.

Closing her eyes to shut out the world for a moment, Jane leaned back and drew a deep breath. She was going on an adventure, and it was going to be fun. Except nothing about this trip had been fun so far. Few things were when they were done in anger.

"Excuse me?"

Jane opened her eyes and glanced up to find an elderly woman regarding her with a kind smile.

"Yes?"

"Do you mind if I sit with you?"

"Not at all," Jane lied, gesturing to the opposite pair of seats in a manner meant to invite.

So much for solitude.

The woman thanked her and sat before promptly retrieving a pair of spindly knitting needles from her bag. "My name's Mandy," she said as she set to work on whatever it was she was making. A sock perhaps, judging from the size of the ribbing.

"Jane."

Mandy nodded and said nothing further, the soft click of her needles filling the silence until the slamming of doors and grinding of wheels drowned out the quieter sounds in the compartment. A whistle sounded somewhere off in the distance. The occasional person who'd come to see their friend or relative off began to wave, and then the train rolled forward, gathering speed as it pulled out of the station.

"So where are you heading?" Mandy asked five

minutes later, dashing Jane's hopes of avoiding conversation.

She glanced away from the brick buildings now streaking by in a blur. "To Cloverfield."

Understanding flooded Mandy's features. She nodded. "A fine tourist destination indeed. There are plenty of ancient burial mounds nearby if that's the sort of thing you're interested in. Or there's the glass blower where you can have a go at making something yourself. I did that once and really enjoyed it."

Jane shrugged one shoulder. "It's more of a research destination actually," she confessed, darting a glance out the window. The buildings gave way to more vegetation and trees as they passed through the suburbs. "I want to visit a real English manor and Summervale House near Cloverfield has been highly recommended."

"It's certainly very fairytale-like." Mandy looped the yarn around her finger and started on a new row of stitches. "So that accent of yours…American by any chance?"

"Yeah. I just flew in this morning, actually. Still trying to adjust to the time difference."

Not that Mandy was likely to care about that bit of information. Jane was simply making smalltalk now, though she wasn't sure why. When she'd set out from JFk airport last night. she'd been too upset about the previous day's argument with Geoffrey to consider talking to a stranger. Which was why she'd been blunt to the point of rudeness when the gentleman sitting beside her on the plane had inquired about her reason for going to England. He'd wanted to chat. She hadn't. Until now, when a charming woman decades older than herself had drawn her into conversation. For reasons Jane couldn't explain, Mandy made her want to open up – to unburden some of her riotous feelings.

"I'm a writer," Jane said while Mandy knitted away. "An author actually."

"Oh? Any chance I've read your work?"

The twinkle in Mandy's eyes prompted Jane to chuckle. "I don't know. My full name's Jane Edwards. I write historical romance novels, mostly set in Regency England."

"Then Summervale really is the right place for you to be heading. If I'm not mistaken, it dates back to the seventeenth century when the first Earl of Camden built it with the intention of using it as his summer residence. He was so fond of the place that he rarely resided anywhere else once it was finished."

"Do you know if his heirs still own it?"

Mandy shook her head. "Sadly, they were forced to part with it years ago when they couldn't afford the upkeep. Happens too often these days, unfortunately." She sighed just enough to convey her regret before applying a more uplifting tone as she said, "But, you'll find heaps of inspiration for your books there though I have to say I've not heard of you as an author. Perhaps if you jot down some of your titles for me, I'll be able to look them up?"

Jane smiled. She appreciated Mandy's kindness. "I'd be happy to." She reached inside her purse and pulled out her notepad, then paused. "Thank you for this."

Mandy tilted her head. Laugh lines crinkled around her eyes. "For what?"

"For taking my mind off of things." When Mandy said nothing, Jane gave her attention to the notepad and wrote down the names of her three favorite books. She handed it over and waited a moment, struggling with the decision of whether or not to share her troubles with this woman she'd only just met.

Inhaling deeply, she chose to forge ahead.

"I broke off my engagement two days ago and booked a ticket to England before I could change my mind." It had been a mad decision prompted by a broken heart and other emotions she'd yet to untangle.

Mandy set her knitting aside and gave Jane her full attention. "You ran away?"

"No." *Yes.* "I don't know. My fiancé and I had a fight which ended badly." Clasping her hands together Jane recalled Geoffrey's angry accusation. *This hobby of yours has destroyed us Jane. When will you realize you can't survive on your stories? And now you want to go to England? Do you have any idea what such a trip will cost?*

Guilt and doubt and the hollowness she'd felt in response to his lack of belief in her, had been like a punch to the gut.

"He didn't approve of my writing or of the genre in which I write. In the end his lack of support and my unwillingness to sacrifice what I love for our relationship tore us apart."

"So here you are. Protesting his opinion."

Jane didn't comment. Perhaps because she knew Geoffrey had a point. Her books had not been selling as well as she'd hoped. Her royalties were barely enough to get by on, never mind enough to help

Geoffrey with the down payment on the home they'd been hoping to buy before the wedding. Without her chipping in, the cute little house in the suburbs had remained but a dream. And Geoffrey had resented her for it. He'd said as much.

"Maybe it's best this way," Mandy said, pulling Jane back to the present. "Perhaps this trip will give you a fresh perspective or even a new beginning. Perhaps it will lead to that bestselling novel you've yet to write."

Grateful for Mandy's positive outlook, Jane smiled. "Yes. Perhaps it will." If such a thing were possible, she'd certainly welcome it with open arms. Because if there was one thing she desperately needed right now, it was to prove Geoffrey wrong.

In the meantime, she meant to enjoy every moment of her visit to England. She already looked forward to drinking tea in the afternoons and going for walks in the historic village where she would be staying. The pictures online featuring thatched roofs and cobblestone streets had been inviting. So had the quaint old posting inn where she'd booked a room.

It was well after lunch by the time she arrived at Cloverfield station. Saying goodbye to Mandy with a promise to stay in touch, Jane climbed down from the train and set out on foot, wheeling her suitcase behind her. The inn wasn't far, no more than a five minute walk, and she was grateful for a little exercise after sitting for hours. She also enjoyed her first glimpse of the village bakery and bookshop and made a mental note to visit both right after taking a look at Summervale.

After a short walk, Jane stepped inside the Hound's Tooth Inn, where a friendly gentleman old enough to be her father showed her up to her room. As with the rest of the inn, history vibrated all around the chamber, clinging to the antique furniture and the worm-eaten beams above her head. It was perfect. The view of Summervale House from her bedroom, more so, with its sweeping façade a sprawling front lawns firmly nestled between the surrounding fields in the distance.

"How far is it?" Jane asked the man, who remained in the doorway.

He seemed to consider. "Perhaps a twenty-minute walk."

His response sent a wave of energy through her. It was only two in the afternoon. She had plenty of time to take her first look at the manor she'd crossed the Atlantic to see. "In that case, I'll come down for a bite to eat before setting out." She was actually starving. "The room is splendid. Exactly what I hoped for."

"Glad to hear it, luv. My name's Mr. Barnes, by the way. Once you've settled in, I'll introduce you to my wife. She makes excellent fish and chips." He left with a nod, closing the door snuggly behind him.

Jane turned back to the window and stared out past the neat little cottages and toward the grand estate in the distance. History was there along with cartloads of inspiration. She could feel it calling to her, demanding she go and explore it as soon as possible.

But not without freshening up first. In fact, a shower would likely work wonders. As would a change of clothes. It was certainly one extra thing she could do to put Geoffrey out of her mind. So she unzipped her suitcase and threw it wide open while trying not to think of the man who'd walked away from the life they'd dreamed of sharing.

She'd made it easy for him when she'd said she was going to England whether he liked it or not. Because in one of those crazy moments, when clarity flashed through her mind, she'd realized one thing. England mattered. Summervale mattered. She needed this trip, and if he could not see that, if he could not support her decision to go, then he wasn't the right man for her. Because he hadn't asked her to be sensible, to wait a little and get the house first and perhaps take a job and write in the evenings. A suggestion like that would likely have cut through her stubborn decision. But no. He'd made her choose. Him or the writing. She could not have both. Which meant he couldn't have her.

Still, it hurt that it had come to this, the realization she did not really know the man with whom she'd been planning to spend the rest of her life. As it turned out, she hadn't really known herself either. She would not have thought herself able to toss such a meaningful relationship aside in the blink of an eye, pack her things and get on a plane, all within a few short hours.

But here she was. In England. Without Geoffrey. She'd even checked her phone to see if he'd tried to call her or text her, but no, there was nothing but silence. Which was probably for the best. After all, what more was there to say without making matters worse? He would move on and so would she. Which meant they'd been wrong for each other right from the start, no matter how much they'd loved each other. But sometimes love was not enough.

Riffling through her things, she grabbed some clean underwear and went to run the hot water in the bathroom. At least if this trip paid off, she'd feel better. If it led to a bestselling novel, that would be great! She would send Geoffrey an autographed copy then and sign it with a smiley. That would show him not to doubt her.

Of course, the problem was she had begun doubting herself. Her lack of success had made her question how long she could stay the course before having to give up her dream of making a living as a full-time author. Geoffrey, as blunt as he'd been, had only spoken the truth – a truth she'd been trying desperately hard to ignore. But having him lay out the facts and force her to acknowledge them had been painful.

Sighing, she undressed quickly and stepped under the shower, savoring the soothing feel of the water splashing over her body. Geoffrey was in the past now. Their argument was just an excuse to end a relationship that had been over for months. The spark was gone and she…she would not think of him anymore. At least not while she was here. The problems she'd left in New York could wait until she returned.

With this in mind, she pushed all thought of her broken engagement from her mind and thought of Summervale while washing her hair and rinsing off soap. What must it have been like to live in such luxury, surrounded by servants and vast amounts of wealth? She chuckled softly and shook her head while turning off the tap. She would not want any of those things if it meant giving up on modern plumbing and all the other conveniences one could enjoy in the twenty-first ^{t} century. Like toilet paper and Wi-Fi. She reached for a towel and laughed. Of all the things to pop into her head first. Wi-Fi. Really? Would it not be better to mourn the loss of antibiotics?

After drying her hair and getting dressed, Jane grabbed her purse and went downstairs to enjoy a plate of the fish and chips Mr. Barnes had recommended. It was delicious, dissolving in her mouth like butter and perfectly complimented by a pint of pale ale.

Thanking her hosts for the perfect meal, she headed out toward Summervale. Excitement buzzed in her veins with every step she took, the prospect of actually stepping inside this magnificent edifice quickening her pace. She'd written about such buildings countless times, her imagination crafting them and transposing them onto the pages of her novels. They'd made the backdrops of all the balls she'd written about. They'd been the homes of her heroes and heroines. But she'd never actually visited such an extravagant place before. Her descriptions had always relied on pictures alone, not actual experience.

Until now.

Leaving the village behind, Jane followed the winding road. She loved how neatly the hedges were trimmed and the colorful display of wildflowers dotting the fields on either side. Although it wasn't the most practical thing to wear when out walking, she'd chosen to put on a long floral dress with pretty puff sleeves and her ballerina flats. It was more romantic than jeans and sneakers and would perhaps more easily allow her to feel a connection with the past. Fanciful thought that, but there it was.

The walk turned out to be longer than she'd expected. Thirty minutes at least. But when she arrived, she had no regrets. Coming here was worth every dollar she'd spent. The impressive façade of Summervale rose, a feast for the eyes with its columns and trim and sweeping front steps leading up to the largest front door she'd ever seen. Flung open, it invited her into a tall foyer where a woman roughly her own age stood behind a front desk.

Jane moved toward her and the woman looked up from the book she was reading. "Welcome to Summervale House." She gave Jane a broad smile and produced a pamphlet. "Are you interested in taking a tour of the manor?"

"Absolutely." Rummaging through her purse, Jane produced the three pound admission fee required and handed it over to the woman, accepting the proffered pamphlet in return.

"We close in another couple of hours," the woman said, "which should give you just enough time to see all the rooms and the garden. As long as you don't read every information piece along the way."

Thanking her for the information, Jane crossed the black and white marble tiled floor while craning her neck to admire the coffered ceiling. Flowers had been painstakingly carved into the gleaming wood, not by machine, but by hand, in a magnificent display of craftsmanship.

Retrieving her cellphone from her purse, Jane took a picture before heading down a wide corridor with rooms on either side. She entered the first one on her left and immediately froze on a sharp inhalation of breath. This was so much more than she'd ever expected, a parlor dressed in blues and creams, with silk upholstered chairs threatening to make any antique dealer salivate.

It was tasteful and had been, according to the sign on the wall, decorated by Lady Tatiana, the tenth Earl of Camden's sister. A portrait of the lady in question hung upon the wall above the fireplace. She'd been a beauty, her dark curls framing an oval face with inquisitive eyes and a pretty smile. Jane sighed, aware the woman had died no more than a year after this very portrait had been painted. How such an event must have darkened the mood within these walls. And yet right now, with the sun gleaming in through the windows bathing the room in a golden glow, it was easier to imagine a lively tea-party or perhaps a romantic assignation taking place.

Grinning, Jane shook her head and moved on. Of course she'd be considering the perfect place for a young, enamored couple to slip away for a moment or two in private. Or a seemingly innocent place for a scoundrel to lure a woman into seduction, as was often the case in the books she wrote, even though reality had likely been less scandalous than that. Finding a portrait of a handsome young man in the library, she doubted he had been anything other than civil. Not at all the classic romantic rogue, judging from his looks, but rather a gentleman through and through.

She studied his facial expression, the deep intensity of his gaze, before reading the bronze inscription attached to the frame. Lord Camden himself had been just as fetching as his sister was pretty. His lips edged slightly toward the left where a dimple added a boyish element of charm to his otherwise serious demeanor. Dark hair fell across his brow, accentuating the deep blue eyes that held her in place.

Jane tried to steady her breathing, yet her heart beat as though he were just as real as she, as if he were actually watching her, holding her captive with his presence. *Ridiculous.* The man had been dead for almost two hundred years. And yet, a deep ache filled her. Logic told her she was being silly, but there was no denying the strange regret and feeling of loss now swamping her.

Intent on shaking it off, she tore her gaze away from him and resumed her tour. Each room proved more impressive than the last, the dining room set as though guests were expected to arrive at any moment. Taking note, Jane jotted down her impressions in the notebook she'd brought along. She could already envision her next novel, bringing Summervale back to life. Her characters would find love here amidst this opulent splendor. And the garden! Spotting the finely kept flowerbeds and walkways, Jane headed toward a pair of French doors and walked out onto the wide expanse of terrace. It was the perfect setting for a masquerade ball and…was that a folly over there? Jane stared. She'd read about these creative structures paying tribute to either medieval or ancient times. This one in particular appeared to consist of a Roman or Greek ruin.

Hastening down the steps to the gravel path below, Jane ignored the gathering clouds now obscuring the sun and the increasing chill in the air. Instead, she all but ran toward the man-made ruin, not halting until she was able to reach out and touch one of the fallen columns. She snapped another picture and admired the work. It would have provided the Summervale residents and their guests with a very romantic destination for their afternoon walks. Perhaps the earl had taken a young lady here to declare his feelings for her? Jane knew he'd never married, and yet she could not help but wonder.

Her chest tightened in a puzzling way she could not explain. Recognizing the feeling, the surge of envy that clawed its way through her, she cast the thought aside. What on earth was wrong with her? What reasonable woman would feel any jealousy for a potentially fictitious girl who'd lived in a different century than herself?

Shaking her head, Jane started back toward the manor. Her breakup with Geoffrey had obviously affected her more than she'd thought. Because here she was, visiting an English manor and falling for a man from a bygone age – a man she didn't even know anything about.

A drop of water fell on her hand, then another as she turned to snap some more photos of the folly, and another still as she put her phone back in her purse. Before she knew it, the clouds were spitting with increased fury until they suddenly split apart, drenching her in seconds.

Where on earth was the sunny sky from an

hour ago? It seemed unfathomable for a climate to change this drastically in such short time, but apparently it had, so rather than ponder the impossibility of it, Jane started to run. Her flats hit the gravel, crunching it beneath her feet as she darted straight for the terrace. It was going to be a long walk back to the village if this rain persisted, but perhaps the manor had a cafeteria where she could stop for a hot cup of tea until it passed.

She was almost at the steps, water streaking over her head, when a crack of lightning tore through the air, the silver-blue glow spearing the ground before her. Gasping, Jane came to a halt. Then a bellowing rumble descended upon her. It was followed by a thunderous roar that propelled her forward once more and with such great haste that the tip of her shoe caught the edge of the step and she tripped. Another flare of lightning lit the sky and flickered across the terrace as Jane went down, dropping her purse in order to break her fall with her hands. And then the world exploded with light, and Jane bent her head to brace herself against the thrashing wind.

The stone slabs were cold and wet beneath her palms, and her knee ached in response to the hard landing it had endured. With droplets of water sliding rapidly over her face, Jane waited until the storm had eased a little, then rose and bent to pick up her purse. But it was gone. She blinked, searching the steps but finding nothing. Perhaps it had fallen into one of the flowerbeds? She started to go and look when lightning zigzagged its way through the air before her, and she hastily turned away with a new thought in mind. She would seek shelter first and look for her purse later. Because if there was one thing she didn't plan on doing, it was getting struck by lighting and dying on the steps of Summervale House.

So she started back up the steps with the skirt of her dress tangling around her legs, impeding her progress. Darkness descended once more, resembling night rather than day and obstructing Jane's vision. Still, she continued forward, so eager to get inside that she almost tripped once again, this time over the body blocking her path.

With a jolt, her heart slammed against her chest. A chill pricked her skin. Dear God. Was that..? She swallowed hard, rain streaking over her hair and shoulders as she stared down at the twisted limbs. The glow of occasional lightning eerily highlighted details: an expensive gown draped over a female form, long hair spread out on the shimmering granite slabs, a face Jane had seen only a short while earlier.

No.

It can't be.

And yet, she recognized Lady Tatiana's appearance immediately, the blood pooling close to her neck as real as the wetness numbing Jane's bones. Shouts sounded from inside the manor. They were followed by the thud of footsteps approaching at a rapid run. The French doors flew open and several people appeared. Jane stared, her attention now fixed on the man who marched toward her. His face conveyed his fury, the rage he would no doubt unleash upon her at any second. It bore no semblance at all to the charming expression conveyed in his portrait.

Although her mind struggled to accept the reality of it, Jane knew who he was in an instant. Not an actor, but the actual Earl of Camden himself, in all his aristocratic glory.

"I will have you hanged for this," he snarled while glaring down at her upturned face.

Jane flinched. "What?" She'd been so dazed by the strangeness of the situation in which she found herself, her mind attempting to comprehend it – to logically explain it – she'd forgotten about Tatiana and how her own presence would likely be construed.

"Who are you?" Camden demanded while two other people remained a few steps behind him. His hands gripped Jane's arms, shaking her slightly as if to force her to speak. And yet, in spite of his obvious hatred toward her in that precise moment, she could not help but appreciate his strength. Which was probably the most useless thing for her to be thinking about at the moment.

"I'm…" Jane stared at him through the falling rain. This wasn't possible. It simply wasn't. And yet the evidence was in Tatiana's lifeless body, the blood, and the very real earl who addressed her. "What date is it?"

Camden's brow knit with obvious frustration. "Are you mad?" She shook her head and his grip on her tightened. Turning, he addressed one of the men behind him. "Take her to my study, Hendricks. Keep an eye on her until I arrive."

Without further ado, Jane was handed over and led away. If she had indeed been transported back to 1818, she dared not think of what might be in store for her. Tatiana's murder had never been solved, the villain never found, yet Jane was now the prime suspect, and she had no idea how she was going to change that without convincing everyone here that she belonged in Bedlam.

CHAPTER TWO

JAMES WATCHED HIS BUTLER ESCORT the blonde haired beauty inside. His eyes lingered on her retreating figure until she was gone from his view. Whoever she was, she'd looked shocked and confused when he'd found her, prompting him to wonder if perhaps he'd been wrong to accuse her.

No.

He shook his head and gave Tatiana his full attention. When he'd heard a scream, he'd rushed from his study to discover what had happened. Snypes, who served as both valet and secretary, had followed. As had Hendricks. Crouching down beside his sister, James ran his fingers gently across her frozen brow. He didn't bother to hold back his tears, allowing them to mingle with the falling rain. It was difficult to comprehend her reason for being out here in such inhospitable weather. Especially since she'd told him she planned to retire for the evening no more than half an hour earlier. Finding her here like this made no sense, which only made the tears fall faster. She'd been his responsibility, his little sister, and he had failed her. Whoever had caused this would suffer the full extent of his wrath, regardless of whom they might be. He would certainly not allow a pretty face to distract him from his purpose.

Curling his fingers into a fist, he rose with renewed resolve. Mourning Tatiana would have to wait. For now. Convicting her killer and seeing justice served was now his first priority. So he rose to face Snypes, who'd stayed a respectable distance away in order to allow James the privacy he needed. "Please take her upstairs to her chamber. Ask her maid to make her look presentable. I don't want anyone else to see her like this."

"Of course, my lord." Snypes hesitated, then said, "I am so sorry for—"

"Just see to it."

The valet inclined his head and James left him to it, trusting the man to complete the task with the same degree of competence he applied to everything else. He then made his way upstairs to his own chamber for a change of clothing.

Once alone, James unbuttoned his jacket with trembling fingers and tossed it aside. His shirt and breeches followed, torn from his limbs with angry movements until he was standing before the mirror in a portrait of crazed undress. *So much blood.* It filled his vision, the memory of it constricting his breathing and tightening every muscle in his body.

Without thinking, he slammed his fist into the crystal before him, shattering his image in a shower of glass. "Aaaargh!" The ache in his knuckles was welcome. The tension released more so. But it wasn't enough. He still felt weighed down and buried alive.

Drawing a breath, he forced himself to regain his

focus. Allowing himself to drown in his grief was not an option. Not if he was to solve Tatiana's murder with a clear head.

With this in mind, he crossed to his chest of drawers with renewed purpose and pulled out a clean shirt and fresh trousers with waistcoat and jacket to match. Once dressed, he descended the stairs and strode swiftly toward his study where the mystery woman awaited. Entering the room, he found her sitting in one of the armchairs close to the fireplace while Hendricks stood by the door keeping watch.

"Have you learned anything?" James asked his butler.

"No. She has not spoken a word yet."

Eyeing her carefully, James studied the tilt of her chin and the gleam in her eyes. Defiance prevailed though he'd yet to determine if it was genuine or a mask she wore to hide her fear. "You may leave us, Hendricks. I will ring for you if further assistance is required."

"Are you quite certain?" Hendricks asked. "She is a young woman and—"

"Possibly guilty of slitting Tatiana's throat," James snapped. "Propriety be damned."

Hendricks visibly bristled but James refused to apologize. He waited until the servant had shut the door behind him before turning back to his quarry. She stared at him with undeniable interest, her dark brown eyes framed by long black lashes assessing him in a manner that quickened his pulse and caused irritation to flare.

"Who are you?" he clipped, repeating the question from earlier.

She tilted her chin and crossed her arms. "Jane Edwards."

Frowning, he ran the name through his mind. It was plain but unfamiliar. "Where do you live?" Something about her was off. She seemed out of place somehow, her dress an entirely different cut from any other he'd ever seen. And her hair had not been styled or hidden beneath a bonnet. Instead, the loose tresses fell over her shoulders and down her back in an untamed manner that stirred his imagination. And not in a good way, all things considered.

"I cannot say."

"Why not?"

"Because the truth is quite unbelievable. Considering the situation I am presently in, I would like to avoid being thought of as crazy."

Her cryptic remark piqued his interest even though it annoyed him. What he needed right now was answers, and she seemed reluctant to provide him with any. But blustering as he felt inclined to do would probably not help. So he searched his mind for a different angle from which to approach her and immediately focused on the manner in which she spoke.

"You sound as though you are forcing your words." He studied her, registering the momentary spark of acknowledgement in her eyes. "So I presume you are not from around here. Perhaps…" he continued as he moved closer to where she sat, "you are not even British."

Her jaw tightened with visible defiance. She averted her gaze and James reached out, catching her chin with his hand and forcing her to look at him. "Are you a spy?" He couldn't imagine why she would be since he and his sister did not have any secrets worth ferreting out. Which led him to his second question. "An assassin?"

The edge of her mouth twitched. And then she suddenly laughed.

James stiffened, caught between anger and complete incredulity. He dropped his hand and leaned toward her with intentional menace. "You find this amusing?" He knew the lethal tone in his voice was intended to make pure fear run through the veins of those on whom he chose to use it. So he was not surprised when his visitor flinched as though she'd been slapped.

"No. Of course not." All humor vanished from her features. "I am not a spy or an assassin. I am an author and I did not kill anyone."

An author? James stared at her, momentarily lost in the depth of her dark brown eyes, so full of compassionate kindness right now, he regretted the moment she glanced away. "Why should I believe you?"

"I don't know."

"That is not very helpful, Mrs. Edwards."

"*Miss*, if you please, and I'm sorry I can't tell you more. All I can do is give you my word that I am innocent in this."

He winced. "You do understand that there is no other suspect, that you appeared out of nowhere, standing over my sister's body, and you would have me *trust* you?" His voice was rising out of frustration, but he could not seem to control it. Never before had he felt so helpless, and with Miss Edwards offering no information, she served as a hindrance more than anything else, which only increased his annoyance. "Do you take me for a fool?"

Her eyes widened. "No. Of course not. It is just…" She swallowed and seemed to consider how to proceed. When she spoke again, her words were measured. "I didn't expect to arrive here this evening. Finding your sister's body was quite a surprise. I'm sorry about what happened to her. Truly."

James clenched his fists. "I never said who the woman was, and yet you know she is my sister?"

Miss Edwards dropped her gaze to the floor and drew a shuddering breath. "I cannot explain."

"I insist you bloody well try!" He'd never cursed in front of a woman before, but this one pushed him past all restraint.

A tortured bit of laughter escaped her. Raising her chin, she regarded him with utmost seriousness. "Very well. Considering her age and the silk gown she was wearing, I made an assumption. Apparently it was correct."

Narrowing his gaze on her, James tried to discern if she was indeed being honest. He wasn't sure. If she were, there was still the matter of her presence to consider. "Even if what you say is true, which I very much doubt, I still want to know what business you had wandering about my property in the middle of the night."

Jane flinched. The earl was furious and rightfully so. But what explanation could she possibly give him without getting locked up for good, or worse, condemned to die? So far, she'd gotten by on her knowledge of Regency England, but it would only get her so far. The man was not an idiot, and she'd be stupid to treat him as such. Which meant she had to give him a plausible reason for her presence along with cause to let her stay. Because while she could not for the life of her comprehend what had happened, she hoped the portal, or whatever it was that had brought her here, might appear again so she could return to her own time.

"I came to seek a position." It was in fact the first thought that popped into her head.

One elegant eyebrow shot up, creasing his forehead. "Why not say so at once?"

"Because the first thing you said when you saw me was that I would hang." Keeping utterly still, she held her breath and prayed he'd believe her.

He did not look convinced. "A position as what, exactly?"

"I don't know but I need the funds and thought I'd inquire." When he continued to stare at her, she slumped back against her chair with a groan. "The truth is I recently arrived from America." Which was true. "The few funds I brought along with me were stolen almost immediately after disembarking in Plymouth, so when I spotted your estate I saw a potential opportunity. That's all."

He narrowed his eyes and peered at her as if hoping to read her mind. The intensity of it, along with the dread of what might happen if he were to doubt her, made Jane's heart thrash about inside her chest.

"So you are American?" She nodded and his frown deepened. "I suppose that explains your peculiar speech pattern and…your strange choice of clothing."

He allowed his gaze to slide over her without apology. A wave of heat assailed her, banishing the chill of her still-wet clothes. In spite of her unappealing circumstance, awareness sparked so acutely, she all but gasped.

Instead, she responded tartly to hide the reaction. "I would have dressed more appropriately if I'd known I'd be conversing with aristocracy."

The edge of his mouth twitched enough to convey a spark of humor. It was gone as quickly as it had appeared, buried beneath his serious demeanor. "Regardless, I have no need for an additional maid. As to what you may have witnessed, however…"

"I saw no one else."

A lengthy pause followed before he turned away and strode to the door. Stopping there, he glanced back at her. "In that case I have no further use for you right now. You will remain here under watch until I confirm what you say is true. If you are indeed as innocent as you claim, you shall be released. If you are not, the magistrate will see to your arrest." He held her gaze for a long second before inclining his head. "Good evening, Miss Edwards. I do hope you enjoy your stay here at Summervale."

He was gone before she had a chance to say anything further. Enjoy her stay? Was he serious? At least if she did remain here there was still some hope she might find a way back to her own time.

Any lingering possibility that the recent events had not been a reenactment arranged by the museum had been dashed as soon as she'd been taken inside by Hendricks. Everything had looked different from how she remembered. The furniture seemed newer and there were pieces present that hadn't been there before, while others were missing. Some paintings had also been moved. But it was more than that. It was that the house now felt lived in.

The door opened and a woman appeared. "Miss Edwards." Her tone was very precise. "I am Mrs. Fontaine, the housekeeper. If you would please come with me, I will show you up to the room in which you are going to be staying."

Unsure of what to expect, Jane hesitantly stood. "I'm very cold," she confessed.

Mrs. Fontaine looked her up and down with a pair of sharp eyes. "Yes. I imagine you would be. The sooner we get you out of those clothes the better."

Jane followed her from the room, quickening her step on occasion in an effort to keep up with the housekeeper's pace. They ascended the grand staircase and made their way along a corridor until Mrs. Fontaine came to a sudden halt in front of a door. Opening it, she ushered Jane inside. "The maid's quarters are full, so his lordship has asked for you to be put in here."

The room was gorgeous, more extravagant than any other she'd ever seen. Pastel shades of blue dominated the space, accentuated by white accents. The furniture itself was extraordinary. Intricately carved, it consisted primarily of a tall wardrobe, a dressing table, and a magnificent four poster canopy bed fit for a queen. "It's lovely."

"I will bring some clothes for you so you can

get changed. A hot bath has already been ordered, though you ought to know that it is only to prevent you from catching your death." Mrs. Fontaine spoke with obvious discomfort and without ever meeting Jane's eyes.

"I didn't kill Lady Tatiana." Jane felt a sudden urgency for the housekeeper to believe her. "I could never do that. I truly hope whoever did it is found and punished."

"Thank you, but until that happens, I intend to remain on my guard."

In other words, she was not about to trust Jane.

"Of course."

Mrs. Fontaine straightened her spine. "And since you claim to have come here seeking employment, I hope securing this room for yourself will not encourage you to forget your position within society."

Jane understood completely. The housekeeper thought her unworthy and rightfully so. Especially considering the time period in which she found herself. "Understood." She added a nod for good measure, hoping to ease Mrs. Fontaine's concerns.

Mrs. Fontaine did not look the least bit relieved but rather than comment, she went in search of the clothing she'd promised, returning moments later with a bundle of white and grey fabric in her arms. "Stays, chemise, dress, and stockings," she said, laying the items out on the bed. "One of the maids was good enough to provide them when I asked. Considering her size, I believe they ought to fit you well enough."

A knock sounded, announcing the arrival of four footmen who carried a tub. They were followed by two more footmen, each bringing a pail of steaming hot water with them. The bath was prepared under Mrs. Fontaine's supervision while Jane stood by, appreciating the cordiality with which she was being treated, all things considered. Surely, if the earl truly believed her guilty of murder, he would have thrown her in a dungeon instead.

Or perhaps his code of honor – something lacking from everyday life in the twenty-first century – compelled him to see to her comfort regardless.

Either way, she looked forward to the bath and was grateful when the footmen departed. "I will help you undress," Mrs. Fontaine said. She took a step toward Jane, who took an immediate step back.

"Thank you, but I am perfectly capable of doing that on my own." Especially since she had no wish for Mrs. Fontaine to see the zipper in the side of her dress or her very un-nineteenth-century underwear.

All of the above would likely shock the woman. She'd probably show it to her master and, as mortifying as that would be, Jane's greatest concern was that he might choose to tell the authorities. Jane would then be brought in for questioning and perhaps lose her chance to return to her own time. It wasn't a risk she was able to take.

Thankfully, Mrs. Fontaine respected her boundaries. "Very well then. I will lock your door for security reasons. If you need something, you may ring the bell." She pointed toward the red velvet rope that hung in one corner of the room.

Jane dipped her head. "Thank you. I appreciate your help."

Without further comment, Mrs. Fontaine departed, leaving Jane to her bath and the myriad thoughts swirling through her mind.

Staring into the fireplace, James downed the remainder of his brandy and muttered a curse. What a God-awful day this had been. His sister had been brutally murdered for reasons he could not begin to understand, and the only person he'd found at the scene was an utter enigma. *Jane Edwards.* A curious woman with secrets carefully guarded behind deflection and lies. Any judge in the land would find her guilty. And yet instinct told him the opposite was true.

He was fairly certain she'd fabricated the story about seeking employment. But then why the devil had she been walking through his garden? What was her purpose for being on the terrace this evening?

Re-filling his glass, he took another sip. Her story bound her to Summervale instead of allowing escape, which suggested she wanted to stay. But why? Unable to figure it out, he turned down the oil-lamps and exited his study.

A quick glance toward the parlor made his chest ache. Tatiana now lay there, surrounded by candles and flowers, while footmen took shifts keeping watch. Mrs. Fontaine had done a wonderful job, preparing her for the upholsterer's arrival in the morning. If they'd been in London, the funeral furnisher they'd used when his father had passed would have been called, but here in the countryside where few could afford such extravagance, the task fell on tradesmen.

Strangely, Tatiana's personal maid had been unable to help since she had apparently gone missing. The girl had not been seen since earlier in the day. Footmen had been sent out to search for her, but Betsy had not yet been found. James could only hope that her absence was not connected to the crime. He rather liked the young maid and her spirited personality and would hate to discover her capable of committing murder.

Sighing, he started up the stairs on heavy feet. Tomorrow he would question the servants again and in greater detail, hopefully with the help of the magistrate Snypes had sent for. A new search party would be sent out to find Betsy, and Miss Edwards would give him some proper answers if he had to wring them out of her himself.

Passing her door, he paused, considering. Light spilled beneath it, suggesting she'd either forgotten her oil-lamp on or remained awake. Would it be improper of him to inquire about her well-being?

Yes!

He hesitated, torn between guilt and anger and an inexplicable need to see Miss Edwards again, if only for a second. Which was wrong. She might still have wielded the dagger that Hendricks had found in one of the flowerbeds. Which was why he'd insisted on making her his prisoner until such a theory could be completely dismissed. But all things aside, he was still a gentleman, and as such, would the proper thing not be to inquire if she needed anything before he retired?

That's what the servants are for.

Yes, but she was still his responsibility and if she

was innocent of the crime…

He rapped lightly on the door. There was a pause and then a very soft, "Yes?"

James steeled himself. "Are you all right in there?"

"I cannot complain. The room is lovely."

"Excellent." He ought to leave it at that and be off, except her voice held him captive, and damn him he wanted to hear more of it, even though he knew he couldn't yet trust her. Caught between the urge to see her punished for the crime she might have committed and the strange desire to protect her if she was innocent, he asked, "Do you have all that you need?"

It was not until the words were out that he realized how propositional they sounded. Which got his mind thinking about things he really should not be thinking about. At all. If only she would say something. Except she didn't. She kept silent for an infernally long moment while he began wondering how best to take his leave and spare them both additional awkwardness.

But then she said, "Some food would be nice."

"You have not eaten?" He could not believe it.

"I did not want to bother the servants any more than I already have and I thought…I thought I could manage until morning, but now I'm suddenly ravenously hungry."

Her comment surprised him. What sort of cold-blooded killer would spare a thought for the comfort of servants? Making his decision, he told her quickly, "I will fetch something for you. It won't take long."

"But—"

He did not linger to hear her protestations but

hurried downstairs to the kitchen. It was well after midnight, so all the staff had retired, leaving him to rummage through the pantry alone. He was used to it though since he often enjoyed a late night snack and was loath to wake a maid or a footman to do a chore he could easily accomplish himself.

Finding a plate, he made an arrangement of ham and cheese, some bread, an egg, and a few tomato and cucumber slices. He then climbed the stairs, returning to Miss Edwards's chamber and knocking gently on the door. "May I come in?" When she answered in the affirmative, he grabbed the key to the room from the hook where it hung on the wall and unlocked the door.

Pushing it open, he entered, and froze as soon as he saw her. Because there she was, sitting on the bed in the plain chemise Mrs. Fontaine had provided and with not just her feet or her ankles but her entire calf showing. The pose was casual, relaxed, and the coverlet mostly tucked around her, but still, he was a man and she…Hell, he could not for the life of him tear his gaze away from the beauty of that limb. The skin was perfect, unblemished and… he almost forgot the plate, straightening it not a moment too soon before the egg rolled over the side.

Irritation followed on the heels of his visceral reaction. Because she'd known he was coming and had not bothered to make herself descent, making him wonder if she'd deliberately chosen to uncover herself in some ploy to provoke him.

Clenching his jaw, he tightened his grip on the plate and glared at her with intentional ire. "You should cover yourself," he clipped.

"Oh!" It was as if his presence had just occurred to her then for she quickly pushed her bare leg under the coverlet and pulled the entire mass of fabric all the way up to her chin. "Sorry. I forgot myself completely."

He chose not to comment and made a point of leaving the bedchamber door wide open while he approached the bed. If she was toying with him, she'd soon be disappointed by his unwillingness to participate. "This may offend you," he said and handed her the plate, "but I must inquire about your situation."

She bit into the egg and James watched while giving himself a silent set down. He could not afford to want this woman. Whatever happened, he had to resist her.

"My situation?"

"You say that you are American, which in and of itself explains your boldness. To some degree. But the carefreeness with which you welcome me into your room while in a state of dishabille makes me wonder if…" He waved his hand as if this would be enough to get his point across without actually asking what he wanted to ask. When she simply stared at him, he finally said, "Are you a courtesan?"

She gaped at him.

"It is a fair question." He would not apologize for asking it. "And since the information you have volunteered about yourself has been rather lacking, I am forced to assume that there is something you are hiding. So, with this in mind—"

"You wish to know if I might bring shame upon your home even if I did not murder your sister."

Rather than look offended as he'd expected she might, her expression conveyed a sense of understanding. "You need not worry, my lord. I am not a loose woman, nor have I ever been married, though I did come close once. In fact, the reason I'm here is because I wished to escape my fiancé."

"I see." Her story made a little more sense now. And the way she told it was quite believable. He was sure she was telling the truth about that, even though she might still have murdered his sister. "And do you expect this fiancé to come chasing after you?"

She shook her head. "No. He has no interest in me anymore, nor I in him. I simply wish to start over."

Which was something he could help her with. "In that case, if you are proven innocent and wish to remain here afterward, I am sure Mrs. Fontaine can find a position for you."

It would keep her close, but to what end? *So you can find a means by which to get her into your bed, you scoundrel.* The thought tore through him with lightning speed. It quickened his pulse and pricked his skin. Christ! She might have slit Tatiana's throat without a second thought and here he was, lusting for her regardless. And with Tatiana lying lifeless downstairs in the parlor.

He ought to be ashamed.

"Thank you, my lord." Miss Edwards tore off a piece of bread and placed the ham and cheese on top. She added a slice of tomato and bit into the sandwich she'd created. "Perhaps you would like to pull up a chair and keep me company while I eat?"

He was tempted, but he'd already stayed too

long. Best to keep his distance from her until he discovered the truth about Tatiana's murder. "It has been a long day," he said while backing away. "So I will wish you a good night instead." He reached the door, sketched a quick bow, and quit Miss Edwards's room before her questioning gaze could stay him.

Locking the door behind him, he expelled a breath he had not realized he'd been holding. She was dangerous. Innocent or guilty, it made no difference when it came to the tumult she was bound to inflict on his life. He pondered this while he continued toward his own bedchamber, the need Miss Edwards had stirred in him as fiery and hazardous as a blazing inferno.

CHAPTER THREE

JANE WOKE THE FOLLOWING MORNING to the reminder of all that had happened the day before. Fresh panic rushed through her veins, jolting her into an upright position. *Oh God, oh God, oh God!* She'd travelled through time and was now the only suspect in the murder of Lady Tatiana. Additionally, she'd sensed a deep attraction between herself and the earl. He'd certainly looked his fill at her when he'd visited her room. Even though it was only her calf that had been on display, his eyes had scorched her skin and left her feeling dizzy.

Which was silly. Nothing could come of it. She was not the aristocratic lady he ought to be pursuing. And besides, his mistrust of her would be a huge hindrance. Not to mention that she had no business inserting herself in his life. In fact, the less the two interacted the better since it would make leaving so much easier when the time to do so came.

Clasping the bedspread, Jane pulled her knees up to her chest and wondered how to proceed. She needed to calm down, that much was certain.

Having her heart race along at a constant gallop wouldn't help in the least. Neither would staying in bed and ignoring the truth.

With this in mind, she got up and dressed, then rang the bell-pull and waited, unsure of what to expect next. Would a maid bring her breakfast or would someone escort her downstairs to the dining room?

A knock at the door a few minutes later announced the arrival of Mrs. Fontaine. "Good morning," she said after letting herself into the room with crisp efficiency.

Jane tried to smile even though Mrs. Fontaine's scowl distressed her. "Good morning."

The housekeeper gave her a once over before saying, "If you'll please come with me then." She gestured for Jane to follow. "There is breakfast for you downstairs after which you're to meet with his lordship."

Drawing a breath, Jane followed the housekeeper through the hallway and down the long flight of stairs while wondering what else she might tell the earl. She did not have the information he sought and had no desire to share any further details about herself for fear of revealing too much. Wasn't that time travel lesson number one? Not to interfere with the past? As it was, her presence alone might cause a serious ripple in the timeline if the movies she'd seen on the subject were anything to go by.

This meant that maintaining her cover as a woman who'd fled a displeasing match was of the essence. And thankfully, Camden had already offered her the chance to stay. Because not only did she have no idea where else to go if he didn't, she was also reluctant to leave the manor in case the portal materialized once again. Staying here was probably her only hope of ever returning home. A prospect she tried to ignore, considering how unlikely it would be for her to travel through time not once but twice in one lifetime. And end up where she belonged.

But since hope was all she had and getting hysterical over her dismal odds would not help at all, she tried to keep a level head. Especially since doing so would make it easier for her to avoid getting charged with a crime she had not committed.

Passing the parlor on the way to the dining room, Jane caught a glimpse of Tatiana. She was laid out on a long table that must have been brought in for this purpose alone, for it looked out of place in the intimate seating space. A footman stood guard near the door to the room, eyes hardening with undeniable contempt as they locked with Jane's. Reminded of her position here, she averted her gaze and hurried after Mrs. Fontaine, eager to have breakfast over with so she could speak with Camden again. Perhaps by then she would think of a way to defend herself against the accusation she faced.

Unfortunately, such a scenario was highly unlikely considering the facts. It was the typical plot she'd seen in a hundred movies where some poor fool was found standing over a corpse, often-times with the murder weapon in their hand. At least the knife the killer had wielded had not been found anywhere near her. But even so, from Camden's and everyone else's perspective, she was the stranger who'd been found in a spot where she shouldn't have been. Convincing them of her innocence would not be simple, especially when DNA and fingerprinting were out of the question. All there was, was circumstantial evidence, and right now, everything pointed to her.

Pushing the unpleasant thought aside, Jane entered the dining room and took a seat at the table. Unlike the tasty meals she described in her books, porridge was the only food awaiting her this morning. She took a few bites, chasing them with a sip of hot tea.

"Good morning, Miss Edwards."

Jane turned to find the earl casually striding toward her. He looked incredibly handsome this morning, dressed in a charcoal grey jacket and black trousers. His hair was neatly combed, making him look more tamed than the previous evening. Although more elegant, Jane decided she rather preferred the messier appearance.

"Good morning, my lord." She set her spoon aside. The porridge wasn't terrible, but neither did it stir her appetite.

As if reading her mind, Camden said, "I thought it best to offer you only a simple meal. Just in case you are guilty, in which case you do not even deserve as much as that."

His suspicion of her could not be plainer. Jane grimaced. "You needn't explain. I understand your reasoning completely." Especially since she'd claimed to be seeking employment as a maid. It was unlikely such a position would warrant better fare than what she'd received.

"Indeed." Camden studied her with no small degree of thoughtfulness. "In that case, if you are done, I would like you to join me in my study."

Jane followed him from the room in complete silence. She still wasn't sure how to prove her innocence. Hopefully inspiration would strike sooner rather than later. "May I sit?" she asked upon entering the study. She would feel better not having to stand.

"By all means." Camden gestured toward the vacant chair that stood across from his desk. Another chair was already occupied by the second man who'd arrived on the terrace last night. "This is my secretary and valet, Mr. Snypes."

Mr. Snypes gave Jane a look of distinct disapproval. "I cannot say it is a pleasure to make your acquaintance."

Jane chose to answer him as bluntly as he had addressed her. "As far as I know, I have not yet been found guilty."

"I believe that is only a matter of time," Mr. Snypes said, "all things considered."

"Enough!" Camden lowered himself to the last remaining chair. "Arguing won't yield any results. What we need are facts."

Mr. Snypes nodded. "Which leaves us with Miss Edwards standing over your sister's body last night."

Forcing herself to stay calm, Jane thought back on all the murder mystery novels and TV shows she'd enjoyed over the years. Perhaps it would help if she could prove she lacked motivation? It was worth a shot.

"I didn't know Lady Tatiana, so what reason would I possibly have to kill her?"

"It is possible that you came here intending to rob the place and she intercepted you. Killing her could have been an act of self-preservation on your part," Mr. Snypes pointed out.

"If that was the case I would not have been dressed as I was. Nor would I have remained on the terrace for you to find me."

"Perhaps you were too shocked by what you did to think about fleeing." This comment was made by Camden, reminding Jane that he did not trust her and that he had no intention of dismissing her as a suspect any time soon. No matter how well he'd treated her thus far or the fact that he'd seemed to find her attractive the previous evening.

He probably felt guilty about that today and was trying to keep his guard up around her.

She clutched her hands in her lap and looked from one man to the other. "May I ask if the murder weapon has been found?"

"It has not," Camden said.

"And you don't think it would have been if I was the one to wield it?" she asked. "Would it not have been on my person or somewhere nearby?"

Both men shared a glance before Camden finally nodded. "A definite point in your favor, Miss. Edwards."

A knock at the door brought Hendricks into the room. "I hope you will pardon my intrusion, my lord, but Harrington and Rockwell would like to speak with you. May I show them in?"

James gave his consent. It had already been a busy morning with the upholsterer arriving before he'd even finished his breakfast. He sighed as he thought back on all the requests he'd made, like for Belgian Blacks to pull the hearse and for them to be fitted with ostrich plume headbands. He'd asked for the coffin to be dressed in purple silk velvet rather than black and for the engraving on the silver breast plate to include a bouquet of violets, Tatiana's favorite flowers.

It had been a depressing conversation, but at least the necessary arrangements were now taken care of so he could focus more fully on solving the crime. Which might be harder than he'd anticipated without the help of the magistrate. Apparently the man had gone away on business and wasn't expected back for another two weeks. His clerk had sent a brief missive, apologizing for the inconvenience.

Uselessness, more like, James had decided while muttering an oath and resolving to catch the villain himself.

At least he had his servants. Snypes would handle the preparations required for the visitation of mourners along with any immediate business dealings. The man had been in James's employ for over five years and was perfectly capable. James trusted him completely, which was part of the reason why he'd asked him to sit in on this meeting with Miss Edwards. He'd wanted a second opinion — some solid feedback. But perhaps that had been a mistake considering Snypes's hostile response to Miss Edwards. His remarks had not been conveyed with the open-minded objectiveness James had hoped for. Rather, it was clear that Snypes had already judged Miss Edwards and found her guilty. Which was not very helpful at all.

"Camden," Rockwell said upon entering the room with Harrington by his side. Both men's faces were set in tight lines. "Is it true? Has your sister really…" He stared at James in disbelief, allowing the rest of the words to remain unsaid.

"It is." James turned toward Miss Edwards. "May I present my good friends, the Earl of Rockwell and Viscount Harrington. They have been visiting me for the past week."

"A pleasure," Miss Edwards murmured. She'd risen, allowing both gentlemen to assess her, which they proceeded to do with unashamed interest.

Bothered by it for reasons he couldn't quite comprehend, James went to pour himself a brandy. Behind him, he heard Rockwell murmur, "Indeed, the pleasure is entirely ours."

To which Snypes immediately added, "Perhaps you will reconsider that sentiment upon hearing that Miss Edwards may be the villain responsible for her ladyship's untimely demise."

"That will be all, Mr. Snypes," James clipped. He cast a disapproving glance at the servant while making a mental note to remind him of his boundaries. James might enjoy his advice, but it was important for Snypes to know when to keep his mouth shut.

A momentary hush followed and then, "As you wish, my lord." Snypes departed, closing the door behind him.

James turned more fully toward his guests. "Miss Edwards's role in all of this has yet to be determined." He invited Rockwell and Harrington to sit, which they did while he himself remained standing. "I made her acquaintance last night when I arrived on the terrace to find her standing over Tatiana's body."

"Good God!" Rockwell stared at Miss Edwards

as though she might threaten to kill him next.

"However," James added, noting Harrington's narrowed eyes, "the murder weapon has yet to be recovered. It was not in Miss Edwards's possession at the time of her apprehension, nor has it been discovered in the garden."

"In other words," Harrington drawled, "she did not dispose of it right before you found her."

James took a sip of his drink, savoring the soothing heat as it slid down his throat. "It doesn't appear so. No."

"Which would mean she did not do it," Rockwell said.

"It is becoming increasingly unlikely," James agreed. He eyed Jane who was looking increasingly uncomfortable. "I still have a great number of questions, however. Ensuring you have no hand in this matter will take time – time you will spend here at Summervale under my watchful eye."

He pinned her with a stare, determined to make her understand the severity of the situation in which she found herself and that he would have no qualms about seeing her punished if she were found guilty. But rather than show defiance or fear, she blushed and allowed her gaze to fall away from his.

"Yes, my lord."

She murmured the words with a touch of sensuality that quickened his blood. Confounded and discomforted by it, he returned his attention to the side table and busied himself with pouring drinks for his friends. Anything to alleviate the wild imaginings he'd started having about a woman he probably ought to despise. Fantasizing about her would be extremely inappropriate.

"Brandy?" He offered a glass to Rockwell and then to Harrington, but both declined.

"We've not yet broken our fast," Rockwell explained while James set down the glasses.

"When we discovered what had transpired, we thought to seek you out first," Harrington said, "but the truth of it is, I am famished."

"Me too," Rockwell said. "So if you do not mind, we will take ourselves off and fill our aching bellies." His brow creased in contemplation, his eyes darkening with sympathy. "Perhaps we can go for a ride later? You look as though you could use a distraction."

James shook his head. "Forgive me, gentlemen, but you will have to go without me. With all that has happened, there is too much for me to attend to. People are expected to arrive later today to pay their respects. I have to be here."

"Of course," Rockwell said. He and Harrington stood. "No need to worry about us. We will keep ourselves entertained." They left the room at a solemn pace.

"Fine friends," Miss Edwards said, drawing his attention back to her. "Have you known them long?"

"We attended Eton and Cambridge together." He wasn't sure why he was letting her draw him into personal conversation, but she was here, innocent until proven guilty. So he took the seat Harrington had vacated and set his half empty glass of brandy on the table.

"You did not offer me one." She nodded toward the glass.

He laughed, surprised by her candor. "English women don't usually imbibe at ten o'clock in the morning."

"Did I forget to mention that I am American?"

He shook his head. "No. Indeed you did not."

"Then perhaps you will allow me to enjoy a glass with you? The last twenty-four hours have not been easy. I believe a drink might help."

Lord, the woman was assertive! He'd never encountered anyone from the working class who would have dared speak to him so boldly. Once again it made him wonder if Miss Edwards was more than she claimed to be. Because surely, even an American would know class difference ought to prevent her from addressing an earl so directly. She intrigued him though, which was why he chose to set the glass he'd intended for Rockwell within her reach.

"Thank you." She took a sip without even wincing. "Excellent vintage."

"You are familiar with brandies?"

She shrugged one shoulder. "My father was a collector and connoisseur. He taught me to appreciate the best varieties."

He raised an eyebrow. "The daughter of a man wealthy enough to indulge himself in such an interest has fled America and now seeks work as a maid?"

"As I said, my funds were stolen, so what else should I do? I will not beg or prostitute myself."

"I should bloody well hope not!" He was on his feet again, striding toward the window, unable to understand why the thought of her lowering herself to such a degree would bother him when he scarcely knew her. What she did to earn a living was none of his goddamn business. And yet, her statement had shot through him, compelling him to forget himself and making him curse in front of a woman for the second time in his life. It was unforgiveable, the behavior he subjected her to.

Shoving one hand into his trouser pocket, he drank deep from his glass while staring blindly out of the window at the driveway leading into the distance. "My apologies. My language just now was inexcusable."

"Please don't worry. It doesn't offend me in the slightest."

The honesty with which she spoke conveyed a lack of pretense he'd rarely witnessed in any woman. It was thoroughly engaging. "Are all Americans so indifferent?"

"I'm really not sure." She sounded pensive now, as if the question puzzled her. "Perhaps there are those who would protest to a man expressing himself so overtly in front of a woman, but I rather appreciate the honesty."

"Honesty?" He turned to meet her gaze.

"You must confess, allowing an expletive to slip, unhindered by the presence of others, is the very epitome of candid communication." She knit her brow. "It is now quite clear to me that you abhor the idea of me having to beg or prostitute myself and that, in the event I am found guilty, you would rather see me dangling from the end of a rope because…" Her sentence trailed off as if she hadn't quite managed to figure that part out just yet.

He decided to help. "Because that would be just." He returned to his seat and leaned forward with his elbows resting firmly on his thighs. "If you are indeed capable of doing the unspeakable, of taking a blade and slicing it neatly across an innocent woman's throat, then you deserve far worse than the hangman's noose. But begging and whoring?" He winced, imagining her in such a scenario. "Whoever you are, you are better than that."

"Hence my reason for seeking an honest job."

Her determination was evident. She wanted to stay, which was yet another point in her favor. If she'd really killed Tatiana, would she not do her best to convince him she must return to her parents or something? Would she not simply attempt to flee?

But she hadn't. Not yet at least.

"Have you ever worked as a maid before?" He doubted it, but felt compelled to ask.

"Not exactly, but that doesn't mean I'm unfit. I'm a quick learner and I need the money." She sounded sincere. And desperate.

Something about her story still bothered him though. "You said you arrived at Plymouth?" When she nodded to confirm this was true, he said, "That is quite a distance away, at least a week's travel by coach."

"I hitched a ride." She held his gaze without flinching.

"You *hitched* a *ride*?" He knit his brow, surprised by her colloquialism and her explanation, which was bizarre at best. "With whom?"

"I do not know. The drivers, for there were a few, were not aware of my presence since I stowed away at the back of the carriages."

"In the rear boots?" He could not help but sound

appalled.

"Yes. Exactly. It wasn't too terrible."

He paid attention to her tone. The manner in which she spoke was different from when she'd told him she hadn't killed Tatiana. If she had really gone through such an ordeal to get here, then surely her voice would convey it. And yet she sounded as though she were telling him of a story she'd once read. It lacked conviction.

Still, he decided to play along, because if this was the lie and her innocence was the truth, then he really did not understand her at all, though he was more determined than ever to try. "So then, what made you stop here?"

Her fingers caught the grey wool of the dress she was wearing and toyed with it while she spoke. "As I said, it looked like the sort of place where a woman in need of a respectable job might find one."

"That doesn't explain why you chose to walk around to the back of the house and enter from the terrace instead of going to the servant's entrance at left of the front door."

"Well, I did try to knock there, but I suspect the thunder must have drowned out the sound." She took another sip of her drink while he did his best to avoid declaring her a liar.

It was no use. The story she'd woven was too unbelievable, and his pride would not permit him to let her think she'd managed to fool him. "I'm not sure you killed Tatiana, but I know for a fact that your explanation just now regarding how you arrived here is complete fabrication."

She blinked and had the good grace to look as

though he'd just caught her trying to rob him. "It's the only thing that makes sense."

"I find that hard to believe."

"Trust me. If I told you the real truth, you would laugh at me and send me off to a home for the insane."

He considered her closely. The way she spoke did not align with someone who'd lost the use of their mental faculties. In fact, she was perfectly capable of carrying a conversation with astuteness, responding quickly and intelligently.

"Nevertheless, I ask that you try to give me the absolute truth."

It was her turn to consider him. She crossed her arms and pressed her lips firmly together. "Are you sure you don't believe that I hitched a ride on a few different carriages from Plymouth to Cloverfield?"

"Quite." Her dissembling was getting tiresome. He wanted answers, damn it!

"Right."

She still didn't look as though she intended to tell him the truth. Which made him want to shake her. Instead he reached for a state of calm that was swiftly leaving his grasp. "Please. Whatever it is, perhaps it can help with the investigation. Because if you did not kill Tatiana, which has yet to be determined, then someone else did, and in order to find that person, I need to know everything that happened last night."

"My arrival here has nothing to do with the crime." She stood and started to pace as though she needed to walk a few miles in order to calm her nerves. "Explaining it will not bring you any closer to finding the real killer."

"I disagree." Unable to sit still for one more second, he stood as well. "If there is one thing I know, it is that solving crimes requires facts, and you, Miss Edwards, are keeping a very large piece of the puzzle secret."

She came to a halt, but not because of what he'd said apparently, but because of something she'd seen. Approaching the bookcase, she reached for a slim leather-bound novel and pulled it free from the shelf. "*Pride and Prejudice.*" She gave her head a wistful shake. "I love to read, and this is definitely one of my favorite novels." Flipping it open, she raised her gaze to his in utter amazement, her eyes sparkling as though she were a pirate princess who'd just discovered a chest full of diamonds. "And it is signed by the author, with a dedication addressed to you!"

"Indeed. It is one of my most prized possessions, which is why I keep it here instead of in the library."

"So you have read it?" Her voice had taken on a dreamy quality that sounded rather alluring.

"Of course. Miss Austen is a friend so it goes without saying that I would read one her books if she gifted it to me."

Miss Edwards stared at James in amazement. Staring straight back, he forced his body to remain calm even as blood rushed through his veins. Her interest, the admiration with which she spoke, was dangerous. It reminded him too easily of the celibate state he'd confined himself to since breaking things off with his mistress, and of the fact that he was presently alone with the loveliest woman he'd ever seen.

Schooling his features, he quoted the opening line. "It is a truth universally acknowledged, that a single man in possession of a good fortune, must be in want of a wife."

Her lips stretched into a wide smile that dimpled her cheeks. "Now you're just showing off."

He couldn't deny it. "It is also a truth universally acknowledged that an eligible gentleman is wise to avail himself of the opportunity to demonstrate his accomplishments."

A pair of sparkling eyes met his. "Are you flirting with me, Lord Camden?"

"Perhaps." He hadn't meant to, but there was something so irresistible about her, he could not seem to help himself. "Just a little."

"I'm sure your friends would advise against it." She returned the book to its spot on the shelf. "As would I."

It felt as though she'd just turned down his suit. Which was monstrously preposterous since he had no intention of letting himself get carried away to such a degree. But the thought that she might not find him as attractive as he found her was bothersome. It niggled at his male pride and put him in a prickly mood.

He crossed his arms. "Very well." She'd captivated his interest though, which wasn't something he could ignore. But she was right about the flirting. It wasn't appropriate by any means. So he decided to try ferreting out more information about her instead. "How old are you, Miss Edwards?"

"Twenty seven."

Tilting his head, he pondered that answer for a

second before asking, "Are you a widow or a spinster?"

She gaped at him for a full five seconds before telling him archly, "I have never been married before."

"And yet you fled from your fiancé." He could not make sense of that. "Are you sure that was wise of you?"

"He gave me an ultimatum, and I decided to choose my writing over him."

It was James's turn to gape. She truly was addled in the head. "I see." It was all he could think to say.

"You don't approve."

It was a statement, not a question, to which he responded with a shrug. "It is not my position to judge you, but in all honesty, I wonder how a woman of your age can turn down a proposal in favor of pursuing her own interests."

"Erm…twenty-seven isn't really—"

"You are firmly on the shelf, Miss Edwards, even by American standards."

She returned to her chair and sank onto it in a despondent way that nipped at his heart. "Perhaps, but Geoffrey was the first man who ever proposed to me, and the first I ever considered marrying."

"Then your decision to break your engagement makes even less sense." Figuring out Miss Edwards was like rebuilding a shattered vase. There were pieces that didn't make sense and some that refused to fit. "As a woman, the easiest way to secure a comfortable life is if you have a husband to support you and offer protection."

"I'm sure that's what you think, but perhaps—"
She broke off the rush of words that formed her

response and bit her lip.

Curiosity nagged him. "What were you going to say?"

"Just that…" she hesitated a moment before offering up a defeated sigh "…maybe your opinion on matrimony is somewhat archaic."

James could feel his forehead knitting tightly together above his eyebrows. "I do not believe they differ much from anyone else's. Except perhaps yours, it would seem."

A knock at the door brought Hendricks into the room, saving Miss Edwards from having to comment on that remark. James made a mental note to resume this conversation later as he waited for his butler to state his business.

"My lord." Hendricks met James's gaze without blinking. "Betsy has just been found."

"What wonderful news!" Relief filled James at the prospect of getting additional answers. "You must take me to her at once."

"My lord—" Hendricks darted a wary look at Miss Edwards.

James understood him at once. "Please ask Mrs. Fontaine to see Miss Edwards returned to her chamber." He turned to his guest. "I hope you can understand the need to confine you until we determine what happened last night."

To his surprise, she did not argue as he'd expected after her confiding her radical views on the need, or rather lack thereof, for a woman to marry. Instead, she went with the housekeeper without complaint, adding to James's instinctual conviction of her innocence.

Determined to remain objective, however, he

pushed this feeling aside and followed Hendricks from the room, a little surprised when they did not head toward the servant's quarter or bellow stairs. More so when the butler led the way outside to the stables.

Apprehension slid along James's veins. His muscles tightened and he quickened his pace. "Why has Betsy not been brought back to the house?"

"I tried to tell you," Hendricks said. "Betsy is—"

But James wasn't listening. He already suspected he knew the answer to his question. It was confirmed seconds later when he entered the stable to find his head groomsman standing next to a large pile of hay. "The stable boy was fetching fresh fodder for the horses when his pitchfork struck this."

James took a step closer and followed the groomsman's gaze. A face had been uncovered – a familiar face with a vacant stare and a blank expression.

"Betsy."

James cursed and closed his eyes for a second while anger tore through him. Whatever she might have been able to tell him would now go unheard.

CHAPTER FOUR

STANDING BY HER BEDROOM WINDOW, Jane admired the landscape. Fields cast in shades of gold by the summer sun stretched out toward the right. On the left, a thicket of trees marked the edge of the Cloverfield woods. She'd seen it on an online map when she'd researched the area she would be visiting. In between, wildflowers bloomed like bright specks of paint scattered on a canvas.

Registering movement, Jane dropped her gaze to the graveled area leading toward the stable court-yard and saw the earl emerge at a brisk stride. His posture, she noted, was stiff, his fists clenched at either side as if in anger or agitation.

As he drew closer, his pace slowed until he came to a halt almost right beneath her window. Tilting his head sharply, he met her gaze with a grim expression that tempted Jane to turn away. She forced herself not to even as her heart started to race, for there was no denying that she'd been watching him and to pretend otherwise would be both dishonest and cowardly.

The moment passed and the earl resumed walking, disappearing from her view within seconds and leaving Jane to wonder once again what her fate might be. He hadn't looked pleased, which did not bode well, considering how politely he'd treated her when they'd parted ways half an hour earlier. But whatever trace of joviality he'd allowed had now vanished.

Jane turned away from the view and went to sit on the edge of her bed. Shaking off the feeling of impending doom was becoming increasingly difficult. For a while this morning, she'd sensed the earl believed her innocent, even if he hadn't believed anything else about her. But being the smart man he was and given all that had happened, she'd been a fool to presume he would not cross analyze everything she said. To tell him the truth, however, had been impossible.

She winced while reality took a firmer hold. As it was, she'd had a heck of a time avoiding modern words and phrases since telling the earl how much her situation sucked or asking him to call the police had been the natural thing to do. In hindsight, she was glad she'd caught herself and refrained. Using twentieth-century speech would only result in additional questions. But this meant making a deliberate effort to talk as though she belonged in the eighteen hundreds, which was really quite exhausting.

Obviously, the logical solution would be to say as little as possible while waiting for another thunderstorm to happen and somehow managing to be in the right place at the right time when it did. She was still pondering the logistics of this when a knock at the door, followed by the sound of a key turning the lock, brought Mrs. Fontaine into the room.

"His lordship wishes to speak with you," the housekeeper said. Her voice was as dry as desert sand.

Jane stood and followed her to Lord Camden's study without any further exchange. She stepped inside and remained standing close to the door until the earl dismissed Mrs. Fontaine and invited her to sit on the same chair she'd used that morning and the evening before.

"Do you still want to work here as a maid?" He asked the question while keeping his eyes firmly trained on the ledger before him.

She quickly nodded. "I will take whichever position is available, my lord."

He raised his gaze slowly and met hers. His mouth was set in a firm line, his expression so hard it threatened to pierce her composure. "I must confess I find your willingness to do what it takes to earn an honest living admirable. Especially since I doubt you have ever done such grueling work before, contrary to what you would have me believe."

"What evidence do you have?"

The edge of his jaw ticked. "For one thing, you are well read. You said yourself that you are an author and you enjoy Miss Austen's works. An uneducated woman with a poor background would not have been able to make such claims."

"My family has fallen on hard times."

"And yet you refuse to marry your way out of this predicament."

"You presume my fiancé was wealthy."

Camden winced. "Of course he was. It's common sense that he would have been since your match was not based on love."

Jane sighed. He was wrong about Geoffrey's financial situation, but only because he was basing his deduction on the time period he was accustomed to. As for love, she'd thought she'd found it, only to realize she'd been wrong.

"Very well. You've discovered the truth about me."

"I hardly think I have even begun to do that, Miss Edwards." He leaned back and drummed his fingers lazily on the top of his desk. "However, as long as you are not hiding from the law or from an enraged husband, you may commence work immediately."

"Then…" She had to be clear on one thing. "You no longer suspect me of killing your sister?"

"No. You could not have done so. It would, in fact, have been impossible."

"Why?" She was now curious to learn more.

Camden knit his brow. "Your interest in this matter is most peculiar."

"I hardly think so." When he continued to stare at her, she said, "There is nothing strange about wanting to know why I have been exonerated."

He shrugged as if acknowledging this as a valid point. "Tatiana's maid, Betsy, was found in one of the stable stalls. You were under constant watch or locked away in your bedchamber after being found on the terrace, which means you could not have been the one who killed Betsy."

"You think she saw something and the killer ensured her silence?"

Camden nodded. "Yes. That is precisely what I think. And even if you had somehow managed to sneak out of your bedchamber and commit the act, which would have been impossible, you would not have managed to carry her over to the stables."

"Perhaps she was killed in the stall itself." Why she pointed this out was really beyond her since it did not help her own situation at all.

But Camden shook his head. "No. She had no purpose there. And it rained that night. The ground was muddy, yet there was not a speck of dirt on Betsy's clothing."

Jane took a moment to try and imagine what might have happened before saying, "So the person who did it carried her to the stall after they killed her?"

Nodding, Camden leaned back in his chair. "Which is not something you would have been able to manage." He pierced her with a sharp look that made her pulse leap and her stomach flutter. "Unless you are unnaturally strong, that is."

"I take it she was not petite?"

Camden's mouth flattened. "She was slim but quite a bit taller than you. Which means she was killed by a man large enough to move her to the stables without any difficulty."

Air whooshed from Jane's lungs on a long exhalation of deep relief. She regarded the earl who seemed to be lost in contemplation. "Do you have any idea who the culprit might be then?"

He blinked. "No. Not yet."

"Perhaps you should make a list of those who would have been physically capable of accomplishing the crime."

With a quick nod, he stood and went to ring the bell-pull before returning to his desk. He had just finished retrieving a piece of paper and readying a quill when a maid arrived.

"Please ask Mrs. Fontaine to come and see me," he said. The maid left and Camden proceeded to write, occasionally pausing to think before continuing, the scratch of the nib filling the silence that had fallen between them until the housekeeper arrived.

Camden set his quill aside and regarded the housekeeper seriously. "It has been determined that Miss Edwards is innocent of any wrongdoing, and that someone else is to blame for Lady Tatiana's death."

"My lord?" Mrs. Fontaine's eyes had widened with surprise.

"You ought to know that the culprit would have had to be a man capable of carrying Betsy from the house to the stables. Until he can be found, we must remain vigilant. If you discover something suspicious or a potential clue, you will bring the information to me immediately. Is that clear?"

Mrs. Fontaine nodded. "Yes, my lord."

"In the meantime, you will take Miss Edwards here under your wing. She is in need of work, so I would like to hire her as a maid. You may give her Betsy's room as soon as Betsy's things have been packed away so they can be sent to her parents with our sincerest condolences."

Mrs. Fontaine's jaw dropped and for a few seconds all she seemed capable of doing was gaping. But then she composed herself and said, "I know it's not my place to question you, my lord, but do you really wish to give Betsy's position to someone else after what has happened? I mean," she hesitated briefly before asking, "is it not a bit soon to replace her?"

Camden stared at Mrs. Fontaine with an unyielding gaze that made Jane feel uncomfortable even though she was not the one subjected to it. Mrs. Fontaine, however, managed to maintain a firm demeanor. She even raised her chin a little, which Jane considered remarkably brave considering her position.

"Betsy was a valuable member of this household, Mrs. Fontaine." The earl spoke with cool authority, sending a shiver down Jane's spine. "She was a person with her own independent thoughts and personality, a woman who enjoyed trying to solve the riddles in the Sunday paper my sister always gave her once she and I were finished with it, who spent her meager savings on buying gifts for others, and whose sense of humor and bright smile brought joy to those around her." He leaned slightly forward and Jane felt her heart beat faster. "To suggest I could ever replace her, like a broken dish or some other trifling object, would be a serious mistake, Madam."

"I—I—Of Course, my lord." Mrs. Fontaine's gaze darted toward Jane who could offer no help whatsoever, before returning to her employer. "I did not mean to cause offense. It is just—"

"We need the help more than ever at the moment, and Miss Edwards is conveniently here and ready to assist. People are expected to arrive at any moment to pay their respects, and then of course there are my house guests to consider.

Harrington and Rockwell are not accustomed to fending for themselves. Their rooms will need to be tidied, the chamber pots cleaned, and..."

Jane had no idea what else the earl said. All she could think of was the chore of having to clean out a chamber pot. Never in her life had she imagined herself accomplishing such a task. And she would have to do it without wrinkling her nose or voicing any complaints, since doing so might make her nineteenth century co-workers raise additional questions she was not prepared to answer.

She was still thinking about this and how best to avoid the task now looming before her when the butler returned to announce the arrival of some villagers who'd come to pay their respects. Expelling a deep breath, Camden stood and told his butler to show the visitors into the parlor.

"If you will excuse me." He strode toward the door without glancing in Jane's direction. "Duty awaits."

"As does yours," Mrs. Fontaine told Jane as soon as the two were alone. "Come with me. I'll give you an apron and a tour so you know where to find everything you'll be needing." Her voice was a little softer than before, though it still held the strictness of a school principal Jane recalled from her youth. "Now that you are a maid, you shall be addressed accordingly, so I will need to know your Christian name."

"It's Jane." Hurrying after the woman, she reminded herself that she was an adult, recently declared innocent, and that Mrs. Fontaine had no reason whatsoever to be anything but cordial with her.

Until it became startlingly clear that Jane was in way over her head. Because she had no idea what most of the items in the housemaid box Mrs. Fontaine gave her were supposed to be used for, nor did she understand what tea leaves had to do with sweeping a carpet. But she supposed she would figure it out as she went along. As it was, she had no plans for an extended stay here, so if all went well, lightening would soon strike again, and she would return to her own time period without too much trouble.

With this piece of optimism in mind, Jane listened carefully while Mrs. Fontaine continued issuing instructions. "You will rise by six in the morning and commence work no later than half past six. The dining room is your responsibility now. It will have to be swept and dusted before the table is set for breakfast. If it is a particularly cold day, a fire will have to be made and—"

"A fire?" Being accustomed to baseboard heating, Jane had never handled an open fireplace before, though she had helped her dad build a bonfire a few times when she was a child. How hard could it possibly be?

Mrs. Fontaine darted a look in her direction while taking the servant stairs down to the kitchen. "Naturally. You'll find all the things you need in the housemaid box I gave you. Except for the cloth to cover the carpet. We keep that on a shelf in the housemaid's closet on the bedroom floor."

"The one where the dusters, brushes, pails, and other housework items are kept?" Jane asked. Mrs. Fontaine had shown it to her a few minutes earlier before heading into the stairwell.

"Precisely." The housekeeper opened a door and led the way through to a low hallway with rooms on either side. "The butler's room and pantry are here on the right. My room is directly opposite, and further along we have the servants' hall, the kitchen, scullery, pantry, and some additional storage rooms for polishing equipment, sewing, and general upkeep."

Keeping silent since she was genuinely at a loss for words, Jane followed the housekeeper through to the kitchen where a plump woman with rosy cheeks busily kneaded a large blob of dough. Flour dusted the counter at which she worked, while another woman nearby washed utensils in a basin from which steam rose in hefty swirls.

"Mrs. Amundson is our cook and over there is Tilly, the scullery maid who occasionally assists Mrs. Amundson with the preparation of larger meals."

Mrs. Fontaine then introduced Jane, adding a brief mention of her duties. She was just finishing up with this when a young woman with fiery red hair tied back in a tight knot came hurrying into the kitchen.

"Pardon me," the woman said as she rushed past with quick steps and proceeded to locate a tray. "People are arriving in droves, so I've come to fetch more refreshments." She started opening cupboards and pulling out biscuit tins.

"It goes to show how beloved Lady Tatiana was," Mrs. Fontaine remarked.

From across the room, Tilly produced a sound that made Jane think she might be stifling a sob.

"What happened is unforgiveable," Mrs. Amundson muttered. "I hope they find whoever's guilty so they can get the hanging they deserve."

The maid, whose movements had been so rushed moments earlier, had stilled. She glanced at Jane with a solemn expression. "Not only for her lady-ship's murder, but for Betsy's as well," she said.

"Jane." Mrs. Fontaine's voice stirred the air. "There is work to be done. Please help Margaret attend to the guests."

"Here's another tray," Margaret said, handing one to Jane. "There are additional cups and saucers in that cabinet over there. Bring as many as you can. And Tilly?"

"Yes?" Tilly replied.

"Put more water to boil. I suspect we'll be need-ing additional pots of tea."

In a whirlwind of commotion, Jane managed to follow Margaret's directions without any trouble. A few minutes later, she was hurrying after her up the stairs while balancing teacups and one full tea-pot on the tray she carried. Pausing for a second in the doorway to the dining room, she thought back on all of the period dramas she'd seen on TV over the years.

Right.

I can do this.

With a quick glance at Margaret, she straight-ened her posture and continued toward the table. The chairs had all been pushed back against the walls so the visitors could circulate more easily and collect the refreshments they wanted.

Setting down the tray, Jane placed the teacups neatly next to the ones already on the table and picked up the teapot so she could be ready to pour as needed.

"Put the tray away," Margaret whispered close to Jane's ear while moving past her.

Of course.

Jane put down the teapot and picked up the tray, removing it to a nearby sideboard. Seeing an older woman collect a teacup, she hurried back over to the dining room table. "May I pour?" she asked as she reached for the teapot.

The woman arched a brow. "You may." She held the teacup toward Jane. "I take it you are newly employed?"

Jane's hand shook in response to the candid observance but managed not to spill. "Yes." She had no idea what form of address to apply and chose therefore to avoid using any.

"If I may, I would advise you to be more reserved. Eagerness is never a good thing, my dear. It conveys inexperience and ambition – an unfortunate combination." She added a slight sniff before moving away, the black bombazine of her gown swishing as she went.

Jane stared after her. "Who was that?" she asked Margaret who was busily folding more napkins and laying them out in a decorative pattern.

Margaret straightened and shot a quick glance at the door before resuming her task. "The Countess of Camden."

Jane blinked. "The earl's mother?"

"And Lady Tatiana's as well." Margaret gave Jane a hard glare. "Now stop woolgathering would you, and pick up that teapot so you can be ready to serve when needed."

Jane did as she was told without arguing, but in

the back of her mind, she continued to try and make sense of what Margaret had told her. There were no portraits of the dowager in either version of Summervale, so her presence had never occurred to Jane. Yet here she was, in the flesh and without any hint of emotion upon her face. Whether or not she'd just lost her daughter was impossible to discern from her expression, which was something Jane considered to be rather troubling.

Realizing the teapot was suddenly empty, Jane hurried back to the kitchen and refilled it. Returning upstairs, she entered the hallway from the servants' stairs and immediately spotted the earl. He was standing by himself in the foyer and looking unbearably lost.

Jane paused. She had a job to do – one she had to accomplish well if she was to avoid getting sacked and sent packing. So she turned toward the dining room where several people were anxiously await-ing her – or rather the tea's – return. She poured for each of them before filling an extra cup and walking swiftly out of the room and toward the foyer before anyone could think to stop her.

"Would you like some tea?" Jane asked the earl. She'd approached him without him seeming to notice.

He flinched as if startled, then focused his eyes on her face. "Hmm?"

"I brought you some refreshment."

Lowering his gaze to her hands, he stared at the cup as if wondering what to do with it before finally reaching out and taking it from her hands. The gesture made his fingers brush over hers, if only for a second, but it was enough to send a dart of heat shooting through every limb.

She sucked in a breath and reminded herself to be reasonable. This man was a virtual stranger, two hundred years her senior and an aristocrat no less. What did it matter if she appreciated the effort he made to know who his servants were as people or that he obviously cared about them a great deal? They were still completely wrong for each other. That much was clear.

And yet, she could not help but feel the strangest connection to him. She was drawn, not merely in the way a woman might be drawn to an attractive man, but in a much simpler and yet more complicated way – as if she'd been searching for him all her life, and fate had chosen to interfere so she could bridge the gap in time in order to find him.

Really, Jane?

You truly are a hopeless romantic!

She started to turn away, to resume the work she was meant to be doing, when he halted her progress with a dry, "Thank you." He took a sip of his tea and set the cup back on the saucer. "No one else thought to offer me anything. Except you."

His gaze was hard and unnerving, but she refused to look away, reminding herself instead of what this man had lost and of how difficult it must be for him to deal with all of these people when all he probably wanted to do was chase after the killer.

"Where are your friends?" She chose to settle on a safe topic, regardless of how forward it was.

"They were here. For a while." He drew a deep breath, expelled it, and sipped his tea once more. "Death is a dull business. I believe they decided to take themselves off for a ride to lighten the mood."

"But—"

"I hope you are not about to suggest it was incorrect of them to do so, Miss Edwards." Camden's eyebrows had lowered a notch, affording him with a studious appearance.

His decision to continue addressing her formally threw her slightly off guard. She didn't understand his reasoning.

"No. Of course not," she lied. "It is hardly my place to comment on their behavior and certainly not my place to suggest I would have done so had I been permitted."

He winced. "The events of the past day or so have made me forget how blunt you can be." Handing the teacup back to her, he stuck his hands in his pockets and tilted his head, just enough to assure her she was being studied with immense interest. "Speak to Mrs. Fontaine in that way and she will likely take the switch to those delicate hands of yours."

Jane's eyes widened and she instinctively took a step back. "Really?" He had to be joking. Except there was not the slightest hint of humor about him.

"Best get on with your chores now, Miss Edwards. The day is still young and there is much to be done."

She nodded while feeling as though she'd just been dropped from the top of a clock tower. He did not want her company, which meant that whatever peculiar thing she felt for him, he obviously didn't reciprocate the sentiment. As far as he was concerned, she was a maid and he her employer. It was best for her to remember that so she could forget about how compelling she found him and put her energy toward finding a way out of the nineteenth century instead.

CHAPTER FIVE

JAMES WATCHED MISS EDWARDS WALK away with mixed emotions. While part of him wanted to find an excuse to make her stay, he reminded himself of how inappropriate that would be, considering her new position as a member of his staff. To take advantage of his authority and impose upon her in any way would not be right. It wasn't the sort of man he was. And yet, he could not deny that there was something between them – a peculiar bond of sorts. Which was why he chose to be so formal with her, avoiding all possible familiarity.

He shook his head. His sister was dead, murdered the previous evening. Finding the person responsible *had* to be his first priority. Not chasing after a pretty woman, no matter how attractive he found her. And yet, everything about Miss Edwards made him want to seek her out and get to know her better. His mind could think of little else, which was laughable. *He* was laughable! An earl smitten by a simple maid. Except nothing about Miss Edwards was simple. Nor was she the maid she so desperately wanted to make herself out to be.

He knew this instinctively. Could tell from

the way she spoke and the manner in which she carried herself. She was educated, well-read and clever. And he, damn it, wanted to discover everything there was to discover about her. He'd always considered logic and mathematical reasoning to be of the greatest importance, so it was only natural that instinct would compel him to try and figure her out. And he knew himself well enough to say with confidence that Miss Edwards was a conundrum that would nag at him until he managed to do precisely that.

"Would you care for some company?" Rockwell asked him later that afternoon when all the visitors had gone. Harrington, who stood at Rockwell's shoulder, regarded James with concern.

Having sensed a need to recover from the busy morning, James had taken himself off to the library with the intention of reading the newspaper. He set it aside on the table next to him now and gestured for both of his friends to join him.

"How was your ride?" he asked while Harrington dropped into an opposite armchair and Rockwell proceeded to pour them each a measure of brandy.

"Refreshing." Harrington frowned as if regretting his choice of word. He cleared his throat before clarifying. "I needed to get away for a bit."

James tilted his head and studied the man he'd known since his first day at Eton College. "There's no need for pretense, Harrington." It was as if all sound was sucked from the room, and although Rockwell had vanished from James's line of sight, he could sense him staring at him with eyes as hard as Harrington's. "I know you did not love her."

Harrington's lips flattened against each other. His hands gripped the armrests. "That is a bloody callous thing to say under the circumstances."

Of course it was, but that was often the case with the truth. "Am I wrong?" James heartily wished he might be – that his sister had actually managed to win the affection of the man who'd intended to make her his wife.

A glass was placed before James. "We've known Tatiana since she was a child. To suggest we did not care for her or—"

"I was doing no such thing," James said. His anger with the situation as a whole was starting to rise to the surface once more. Intent on trying to calm himself so he wouldn't lash out, he snatched up his glass and took a large swallow. "Caring for someone is one thing, however. Love is quite another, and you and I both know that Harrington's intentions toward Tatiana, as noble as they may have been, had nothing to do with the latter."

"I would have given her a comfortable life, Camden." Harrington spoke with the same sharp precision as always. "She would have been happy. I would have ensured that."

"Undoubtedly," James muttered, "but it doesn't change the fact that yours would have been a marriage of convenience, not a love match."

"As if there is something wrong with that!" The outrage Harrington felt was tangible.

"Such arrangements are common enough among our set, Camden," Rockwell reminded him. "In fact, love matches do tend to be the anomalies."

James inhaled deeply through his nose and leaned back. "Yes. Of course they are. I merely…"

He pushed all air from his lungs on a tortured sigh. "I wish it weren't so."

There was a pause, and then, "You told me you approved of the match." Although Harrington spoke with calm deliberation, he could not hide the accusatory tone.

"And so I did." At the time. But how much had changed since then? Altered by the slash of a blade. There were too many conflicting thoughts in his mind right now for him to say the right thing. Or more importantly, for him to avoid saying the wrong thing. So he said the only thing that might prevent any further conflict. "Forgive me, Harrington. I am overwrought by grief at the moment and finding fault where there is none to be found."

"Perhaps it would be best for us to cut our visit short and return to our respective homes," Rockwell said, "You—"

"No." James looked at them each in turn. "In spite of all that has happened, I appreciate the company. Your presence here will help me through this." He swallowed past the knot in his throat before adding, "The thought of your leaving and of how empty the house will feel once you do is unbearable."

But it was more than that. As much as he trusted these men, Tatiana's killer had yet to be found, and until that happened, he would do what he could to stop those who'd been present at the time of her murder from leaving the estate. The events of the previous evening had yet to be discussed in detail, the most mundane piece of information turned over and analyzed. Perhaps Harrington or Rockwell had heard something or seen something that neither man considered important right now but that might prove vital in solving the crime. And if that were the case, James would discover it, which meant keeping everyone close and asking the right kind of questions.

He decided to start immediately by turning to Harrington. "Did Tatiana seem happy to you since your arrival?" When Harrington quietly nodded, James asked, "Did she ever mention a falling out to you? Either with a member of the staff or a friend or someone from the village or—"

"No." Harrington's response was adamant. "She appeared to be in good spirits, excited to make our engagement official at the Hartford ball next month. All she talked about was the gown she was having made and how excited she was for me to see her in it."

"She held you in high regard," James murmured.

"As I held her," Harrington said. "You must not doubt that."

James nodded quietly. "Of course." He eyed Rockwell. "I don't suppose she said anything more significant to you?"

Rockwell snorted. "Our conversations were fleeting and mostly reduced to polite greetings. Her attention was entirely fixed on Harrington. You were lucky to win her, you know. She would have been a devoted wife."

"I do not doubt it." The comment was spoken with only a hint of regret on Harrington's part.

James stood and went to the window. These men were like brothers to him, but when it came to women, both were cold and unfeeling. He should have considered this more seriously before agreeing to let either one of them court his sister. But the match would have been a good one – a socially acceptable one – and Tatiana had been swept away in the fairytale while their mother eagerly encouraged it.

"You might consider questioning that footman of yours, though."

James turned to stare at Rockwell. "Which footman?"

"The one you hired since my last visit. I forget his name. Something with a G, I believe."

"Goodard?" James thought of the pleasant young man whom the butler continuously praised for his hard work and dedication.

"I saw him speaking with Lady Tatiana in private a couple of times. When they noticed me, they quickly ended the conversation and he swiftly left." Rockwell shrugged. "Just something that comes to mind now, since it did seem a touch odd."

"Thank you, Rockwell." James gave him a grateful nod. "I will certainly look into it."

"On a different note," Harrington said a short while later, "we could not help but notice that you have hired the very woman you initially accused of committing the crime."

"A decidedly unwise decision, if you ask me," Rockwell said.

"I agree," Harrington said. "You know nothing about her!"

James knew they had a valid point, but he felt himself get defensive, nonetheless. "Miss Edwards could not have killed Betsy since that would have required carrying her, and she lacks the strength for such a task. Not to mention that she is shorter than Tatiana was. Holding a knife to her throat and successfully slitting it seems impossible now that I have had time to think it over."

"And time to notice how fetching *Miss Edwards* actually is," Rockwell murmured, emphasizing James's unusual choice of address.

James bristled. "What?"

Harrington inclined his head. "You have to admit she is a stunning woman, Camden. Are you sure you are not just ignoring the facts and making excuses for her in order to make her more… available to you?"

"Of course not!" The notion that his friends might suspect such a thing, and the growing awareness of it being truer than he even dared admit to himself, disgusted him. He turned back to the window and stared out at the scenery beyond. "Now, if you do not mind, I rather think I would like to get back to the paper I was reading."

A moment of silence followed before the sound of chairs being moved and the hushed tread of footsteps upon the carpet could be heard. Rockwell said something else in parting – something about looking forward to seeing James for dinner – before the door clicked into place and the room turned into a tomb devoid of all sound.

James stayed by the window, admiring a flock of birds flying in formation. The wind tugged gently at the youngest trees next to the driveway and ruffled the top of the foliage. Just beyond the window, a cat sneaked across the grass as if in pursuit of a mouse.

"My lord?"

Startled, James spun toward the voice and stilled

at the sight of Miss Edwards standing a few paces away. She looked delectable with her flushed cheeks and a few stray strands of hair falling against her face. It was hard not to stare, but he made a deliberate effort not to by crossing to the table where his glass still stood and picking it up for a refill.

"Yes, Miss Edwards?" He poured the brandy slowly, focusing on the amber liquid so as not to lose himself in the fullness of her lips or the damnably enticing way the maid's attire hugged her shapely figure.

"I…I know it's not my place to seek you out and address you, but…"

Hearing the hesitance in her voice, James turned to face her and immediately noted the look of concern in her eyes. Disturbed by it, he set his glass aside and went toward her. "What is it?" he gently asked.

"Well…" Another hesitation tempted him to shake her until the words spilled out of her mouth. He held himself in check instead and waited with growing impatience until she finally said, "I found this between the pages of a book in your sister's bedchamber. Mrs. Fontaine said to clean the grate and not to touch anything else, but I spotted a rare collection of poems the likes of which I've never seen before, just sitting there on the dresser, and I couldn't resist and…and…I'm so sorry." She shoved a piece of paper toward him.

James stared down at it and at the hand that held it while struggling to overcome the disappointment that threatened to swamp him. "You went through her things." He could not stand the idea, the utter betrayal of trust or his own poor judgment of character. "I thought you were better than that."

Her hand dropped so all he could see was the carpet on which they stood and the swirls of creamy tones accented by reds.

"I did not have to come to you," she said, sounding hurt. "I could have pretended not to have found this and simply go on with you none the wiser. Instead, I chose to risk disapproval and your condemnation because I believe this might be important." She turned to go. "I'm sorry I bothered. It won't happen again."

Before he could think, his hand had reached out and grabbed her by the upper arm. She gasped and he swiftly pulled her back round to face him, so close their faces were mere inches apart. So close he could smell the fragrance that clung to her person, a sweet aroma he'd like to spend more time exploring. "Who are you that you would dare to speak to me with such brazen disregard for my position?"

She held his gaze as she stood there, rigidly refusing to back away, her arm stiff beneath his touch. "Someone who will not be cowed by any man, no matter his rank or position." She spoke with conviction. "I've won my freedom and suffered the pain of it. From now on, I refuse to be anyone's subordinate, no matter what my employment might be."

Christ and all his apostles, the woman was a veritable Valkyrie, hell-bent on taking her life into her own hands and answering to no one. He stared at her. As much as his status and education ought to compel him to find such an attitude worthy of his wrath, he could not deny the provocative impact it had on him or how incredibly enticing he found it. Which was why he only loosened his hold a little, rather than letting her go completely.

"You are a rare creature, Miss Edwards." He studied her face, watching while her eyes darkened to a deeper shade of green. Her mouth parted and his gaze dropped to the swift display of her tongue licking across that delicious fullness of her lips. "I am glad you managed to escape your fiancé, for it means you are now here instead, ready to defy me at every turn."

Surprise widened her eyes. "You want to be defied?"

He chuckled lightly. "Perhaps. I am not yet sure. But most importantly, I want to be distracted, and you, Miss Edwards, seem more than capable of achieving that."

"I…" A pulse beat at the side of her neck, and she suddenly looked away.

But James held on. "No. You must not do that." He tightened his hold once more. "Look at me. Face me. Be my equal if that is what you truly desire, and give me the challenge I need."

When she raised her gaze to his once more, her jaw was set, her eyes as hard as steel. They pierced him to his core and made him wonder a million questions about position and rank and why they all mattered when all they truly were, was a fabricated illusion created by men.

"Read this," she said, pushing the paper against his chest, "and let me go."

He dropped his hand immediately and took the paper from her hand. "Will it help?"

"I've no idea, but it will give you some insight you didn't have before."

"In that case, I thank you, Miss Edwards and—"

"Don't." She held up a hand, silencing him in a manner he ought to protest. Instead he watched her take her leave while wondering why he found her so damnably attractive and what the hell he was going to do about it.

CHAPTER SIX

JANE SPENT THE NEXT DAY deliberately avoiding Camden. Not only because the effect he had on her was inconvenient and extremely troubling, or because admitting to him she'd snooped through his sisters things had been a mortifying experience, but because she needed the time and space in which to put her own thoughts in order. So much had happened since leaving New York – more than she'd ever imagined possible – and adjusting to her change in circumstance, and considering the chance it might be permanent, left little energy for anything else besides the necessary work required of her.

"You're not like anyone else I've ever met," Margaret said on the fourth morning since Jane's arrival. She was helping Jane change the sheets in the bedroom where Lord Rockwell was staying. When they were done they would prepare the refreshments for the family and their guests to enjoy after the funeral.

Jane fluffed up a pillow. "How so?"

She liked Margaret and was grateful for all the help the other maid had offered. Especially when

Jane had been so frustrated over not knowing how to use the items in her housemaid box, she'd almost dissolved into tears. It was Margaret who'd kindly shown her how to clean out the grate in the fireplace and how to build a fire correctly without Mrs. Fontaine discovering Jane's inexperience.

Margaret shrugged. "I don't know." She shook out a blanket and spread it across the bed. Jane grabbed the other side of it and helped flatten it out. "You know a lot without knowing much at all. It's odd."

The assessment was apt and indisputable, but Jane decided to try and explain it anyway. "I just never had to do any of these things before."

Margaret gave her a funny look and shook her head. "You must have been well off then with plenty of servants about to do it for you, which makes me wonder why on earth you'd want to lower yourself to—"

"There is nothing wrong with doing honest work, Margaret." Jane straightened and looked across at the woman who'd quickly become her friend. "I am not better than you, and I certainly don't consider doing what you do as lowering myself to anything. Quite the contrary. I've learned so much since leaving America, especially about myself and what I'm capable of."

"Well, I hope you stay, because I like having you around. At least until you finish telling me about all the books you've written." She paused for a second before asking, "You don't suppose his lordship might have some of them in his library, do you?"

Jane almost choked in response to that question. "No," she said on a cough. "I think that would be very unlikely." Deciding to share her stories with Margaret had been a necessary step in maintaining her sanity. It was the only way she could think of in which to preserve a part of the person she was when everything else had to be hidden away behind lies. But her stories, set in the same period in which she found herself, were unlikely to cause a stir while still allowing her to share a true and very important aspect of herself.

"Well, it's probably not the sort of thing he'd be interested in reading anyway. No offence, Jane, but men and romantic novels just seem like a strange combination."

Ordinarily, Jane would agree, yet she could not forget or ignore the fact that Camden prized his autographed copy of *Pride and Prejudice* or that he'd actually read the book and *enjoyed* it. The notion confirmed he had a sensitive side Jane would not otherwise have considered based on his firm manner. But it prompted her to wonder if he'd ever been in love and if so, with whom. Disliking the thought of his heart being lost to a faceless woman, Jane snatched up a rag and proceeded to dust the furniture. She was being silly. That much was clear. Especially since there was no point whatsoever to such contemplations.

And yet, she could not stop herself from saying, "I suppose his lordship will have to marry soon though, regardless of what his romantic inclinations might be."

"His mother has undoubtedly suggested it and will most assuredly do so with increased vigor now that he is her only surviving child. Whether or not she can convince him of the fact is a different matter entirely. Camden has always seemed like the sort of man prone to making his own decisions."

"So then, he has not set his sights on a possible wife yet?" Jane held her breath while awaiting the answer.

"Not as far as I know, but then again, I'm not present at all the soirees and balls he attends. All I can comment on are the ladies who've come to visit here at Summervale, of which there have only been a couple of Lady Tatiana' friends. And that was a long time ago when she was still a child, and they would come here with their parents for part of the summer. As an adult, I believe she saw most of her friends when staying in Town for the Season."

"What about male acquaintances?" She pondered the paper she'd handed over to Camden. *I cannot bear to be apart from you either. The years we spent together remain the most precious ones of my life.*

"As you already know, she was being courted by Viscount Harrington."

"And before that?" Jane turned to face the other maid. "Were there any other men she might have spent time with?"

Margaret placed one hand on her hip and frowned. "Lady Tatiana was a proper, respectable young lady, Jane. I'm not sure I like what you're getting at."

"I'm sorry. It's just... Whoever killed her deserves to be punished. Don't you agree?"

"And asking these questions will help with that how? You're not in any position to accuse anyone and—"

"I still can't stop trying to figure it out." An idea

began to take shape. Jane stared at Margaret. "Did she have a tutor at some point?"

"Well yes. A lot of young ladies do. There's nothing strange about that."

"No there isn't." Returning to her dusting, Jane quietly said, "I don't suppose you know how long he was here or how old she was when he left?"

"I don't know. I think he stayed for about three years, mostly while Lord Camden was away at University. Lady Tatiana would have been roughly sixteen by the time he left."

The perfect age and environment for a girl of that age to fall madly in love with the man she spent most of her time with. Jane wasn't sure if it mattered, but the note did suggest that Tatiana hadn't loved Harrington and that her heart had belonged to another.

"Are you ready, my lord?"

James held Snypes's gaze for a moment, and it occurred to him that his manservant did not look well. Then again, neither did he. He hadn't had a proper night's sleep since Tatiana's death, and the worry of having a murderer on the loose was eating his nerves. But now was not the time to inquire about Snypes's health. So he simply nodded.

"Yes."

He crossed the floor of his study with somber steps, not the least bit prepared to walk behind the hearse that would carry Tatiana's body to the family graveyard.

Passing Snypes, he stepped out into the hallway where Hendricks awaited.

"Here you are, my lord." The butler handed James his black beaver hat, which he took and placed upon his head before turning toward the front door where his mother awaited.

He hadn't spoken to her very much since for the past couple of days. Not since she'd pestered him about doing his duty and finding a wife while people paid tribute to his sister no more than a few yards away. She'd shown no hint of the loss he felt, but rather a cold determination that had done little to win his cooperation. It had baffled him, how a mother could show so little concern over the loss of her daughter and instead push her son toward the altar with the sort of urgency that bordered on desperation.

Unwilling to speak to her now or to have to discuss the matter further, he silently offered her his arm, which she took without hesitation. Together, they stepped out into the grey exterior from which the usual vibrancy of late spring seemed to have vanished. Clouds shielded the sun, their dirty-white color promising rain or at least a drizzle.

Awaiting their arrival were Harrington and Rockwell along with the vicar and a few other people from nearby estates. James guided his mother past them all. He was exceedingly aware of their gazes following his every move as he and his mother took their places behind the hearse which thankfully rolled into motion without delay. The rest of the procession fell into step behind them. James placed one foot in front of the other, willing his body to walk when all he really wanted to do was run. In the opposite direction.

"That maid you hired." His mother's voice broke

the silence. "I do not like her."

James felt his entire posture stiffen, the irritation, the anger, the pain, collide and expand within him. He forced a sense of calm he did not feel, which resulted in a terse response. "You have always disapproved of pretty women, so I am hardly surprised."

She snorted. "To say Jane is pretty is a vast exaggeration."

"That may be your opinion, though I suspect you are merely being spiteful."

"James!" She hissed his name as if he was still the little boy he'd once been, ready for her to order him about and still too young to stand up against her.

But that was no longer the case. He was a grown man now and finally able to see her for the bitter woman she was. But while he pitied her, he had no patience for snide remarks. "Leave Miss Edwards alone, Mama. She does not deserve your wrath."

"You refusal to use her Christian name is surprising. It shows you hold her in high regard. Above the other servants." Her eyes narrowed. "Please tell me you have no designs to make her your mistress."

The comment was almost inaudible, but the precision with which it was spoken made James hear it as though she'd shouted it right in his ear. His head swiveled toward her, his eyes absorbing the arrogant tilt of her chin as she looked straight ahead as if he weren't even there.

"What my plans may or may not be in that regard," he clipped while doing his best not to crush her arm or her hand with his superior strength, "is none of your concern."

She appeared on the verge of responding but must

have thought better of it, for which he was grateful. Further relief filled him when he arrived home
after the funeral without the need to exchange
another word with her. But the brief conversation
had depressed his mood even further, prompting
him to retreat to his study while his friends entertained the mourners who'd been invited to stay for
a small refreshment.

The rest of the day passed in a blur. When Harrington and Rockwell suggested a game of cards at
some point, James declined and his friends eventually chose to leave him alone. They seemed to
understand that he needed some time to process all
that had happened without interference, for which
he was grateful.

Dinner that evening was, as expected, an awkward
affair. Nobody said much of anything, so James was
glad when it was finally over and he could retire.
He woke early the next morning, long before anyone else was up. So he chose to let breakfast wait
and returned to his study instead. The funeral was
over now and he had every intention of resuming
his investigation of Tatiana's murder. Deciding he
could do with some coffee, he rang the bell pull
and threw himself into the nearest armchair. There,
he pondered the situation at hand – especially the
note Miss Edwards had found in Tatiana's room –
until a bold knock intruded upon his thoughts.

"Enter!"

The door opened and the woman who'd managed to entice his longing for a lover's embrace
with no more than her presence stepped in. "My
lord?"

He had not seen Miss Edwards for two full days.

The fact that she'd been avoiding him since their previous encounter in the library had not escaped his notice. But she was here now, as gorgeous as ever with her hair not quite as neat as it ought to be and…Christ, when she said, "My lord," in that way, the things he envisioned…Wickedness had no bounds as far as his thoughts pertaining to her were concerned. They'd grown increasingly lascivious with each passing moment, no doubt on account of his prolonged abstinence, for which his distaste of greedy women was to blame. He was sick of spending a fortune on a mistress just so he could bed her, but it was either that or the choice between braving a brothel or suffering marriage. Neither of which were remotely appealing.

Miss Edwards on the other hand…

"A coffee, if you would be so kind." She seemed to start, no doubt in response to his overly polite tone. But he was aware of the error he'd made in clutching her arm when they'd last spoken and had every intention of making up for it now. "Bring two cups please, so you can join me."

She hesitated briefly, then shook her head. "That would not be appropriate."

"No, but today is one of those days where I feel the need to tell propriety and social etiquette they can go to the devil along with anyone who dis-agrees." He watched her eyes widen and softened his tone. "Take pity on me, Miss Edwards. I find myself in need of a little company, and yours is much preferred."

"Very well then." She bit her lip, worrying that tender flesh until he lost all control of his senses. So he watched without pretending otherwise and allowed desire to spread through his veins like wildfire. "I will return in a few moments."

And then she was gone, seemingly oblivious of the effect she was having on him. The ease with which she was able to stir his blood was troubling since he could offer her little more than the warmth of his bed. Marriage was certainly not an option and yet the idea of it as an option now entered his mind, proving how desperate he had become.

He drummed his fingers restlessly upon the arm-rest while anticipating her return. He was an earl and she was his maid. There could be no future besides the obvious. And yet, if she was more than she claimed, as he suspected she was, then perhaps..? An exasperated breath was wrenched from his lungs. What was he thinking? To marry a woman he'd known for a few short days? The very same woman he had accused of killing his sister, then hired to clean his home? It was the very epitome of madness.

But when she returned and he breathed a sigh of relief, he knew in that instant she would be his — she *had* to be his — in one way or other.

He waited for her to set the tray on the table before quietly saying, "Please close the door."

"My lord?"

Ah, the sweetness with which she spoke the honorific. He'd like to hear her say it as a plea while he... No. He had to control his baser urges. "I wish to speak with you in confidence and given your position, being confined to a room with me is not as unacceptable as you might think." When she hesitated, he said, "You are by your own admission not a gently bred lady whose prospects might be ruined by such a thing. Are you, Miss Edwards?"

She shook her head. "No. I am not."

And yet he could see her reserve, the guardedness with which she held herself now, like a wary creature fearful of what he might do. Which made him regret his candor and wish he'd had the patience to be more decent with her. But this craving he felt to have her for himself without anyone else intruding was so intense he could scarcely think straight, let alone focus on being a proper gentleman. A regrettable situation to be sure, and one that demanded a swift apology.

"You must forgive me."

She stared at him. "Must I?"

He winced. "Your directness slays me, Miss Edwards." He reached for the coffee pot and started to pour while she continued to watch with what seemed like uncertain dismay. "Please. Have a seat."

To his surprise she turned away and for one awful moment, he thought she was leaving. Except she paused by the door, glanced at him over her shoulder, and then quietly closed it to shut out all else from the room.

"What is it you want?" The question was quietly spoken, a mere whisper in fact, yet he heard it as loudly as if she had spoken it clearly.

Be brave, he told himself. Tell her.

"Your opinion," he said, deciding to start off slowly. "Your companionship, if you are willing to offer it. You, if your attraction toward me is equal to my attraction toward you."

Color rose to her cheeks, but she did not look away. Instead, she approached the nearest chair and slowly lowered herself into it. She then reached for her coffee and took a long sip before setting the cup on its matching saucer. "I can give you the first two things, but not the last."

Disappointment flared, coupled with swift irritation. "Why not?"

"Because my situation is far too complicated to allow for any personal attachments."

He smiled, pleased to learn he still stood a chance – that her reason did not deny a mutual desire to explore the passion he knew would exist between them. "Our differing stations would not allow for such a thing anyway. What I speak of is carnal pleasure, Miss Edwards and your friendship."

She tilted her head and offered a dubious look that made him feel slightly stupid. "For you to suppose we can give each other both without attachment is incredibly naïve, my lord." Straightening, she folded her hands in her lap. "Now, if there is something else on your mind that you wish to discuss, please tell me what it is, and I shall do my best to advise you."

James could only stare. He'd been turned down with greater swiftness and efficiency than he would ever have thought possible. And by a maid, no less. He took a moment to contemplate his coffee, then decided he needed stronger stuff to get through the rest of the day and went to pour himself a brandy. "Your objectiveness regarding Tatiana's murder, considering your recent arrival, urges me to seek your counsel." He was thinking as he spoke, suggesting something he'd not yet decided was wise. But it was out now and could not be taken back, so he forged ahead instead. "You were wrong to look through her things, but that does not detract from the value of what you found."

Caution filled her eyes, but she did not stray from the conversation or the apparent embarrassment she felt regarding the subject. He admired that about her – her ability to face any difficulty head on.

"Do you know who the note was from?"

"I have a fairly good idea." He hesitated confiding the knowledge because of the impropriety, but then decided that if Miss Edwards was to offer her opinion, she would have to know as much as possible. "I believe it was written by George Thompson, a man who used to be in my father's employ."

"Was he your sister's tutor?"

James started slightly in response to the accuracy of her conjecture. "How did you guess?"

Miss Edwards shrugged one shoulder. "I asked around a bit. When it occurred to me that a tutor was the only man whose company your sister might have kept for an extended period of time, I inquired if she'd ever had one and was quickly informed that she had. While you were absent, I might add."

"My going away was inevitable. I—"

"I am not suggesting you are to blame for what happened, Lord Camden." She offered a reassuring smile which went straight to his heart, warming his soul and soothing his nerves. "And I am certainly not implying that there is anything wrong with your sister forming an attachment with a man who obviously cared very deeply for her."

James shook his head. "You speak as though you are unaware of class differences. But how can you be? It is common knowledge that the daughter of an earl must marry a man of equal or superior social standing. For her to even consider a tutor – for her to have possibly kissed him is…is…" He searched for the right word – one that would not insult his sister's memory.

Miss Edwards however was quicker than he was. "Unthinkable?" she supplied. "Worse than you considering your maid?"

The pointed look she gave him was so thoroughly chastising, he could not help but avert his gaze from hers. With one simple question, she'd made him feel like a naughty child caught in the midst of causing some mischief.

"It is not the same thing," he told her.

"Why? Because you are a man and thus permitted to do as you please?"

He swung his gaze back to hers and stared into her bright green eyes. "No one is free to do as they please."

"Perhaps not," she murmured, "but you are still free to proposition your maid without anyone giving a damn about it while your sister's reputation will suffer if word of her affection toward Mr. Thompson gets out."

It took a second for James to recover from Miss Edwards's passionate use of expletive. Curiously, it did not put him off. Quite the contrary. He liked the freedom with which she spoke and valued the honesty. "Do you suppose he might have acted on the feelings he harbored for her?"

Miss Edwards stared at him blankly.

James sighed and waved his hand. "Do you think he might have kissed her?"

"I suppose he might have." Her words seemed

carefully chosen now, which James found curious. "It all depends on how much importance he placed on such a kiss, since he obviously failed to come to you and ask for her hand. As I believe he would have done if anything more had occurred between them."

Feeling his chest tighten, James took a sip of his brandy in an effort to distract himself from the pain. He knew what she meant, but to think of his sister losing her innocence to a man more than ten years her senior when she'd been little more than a child was simply too much. Still, he had to consider the possibility.

"He might have been too much of a coward."

"No. Not if he loved her as much his note suggests." Miss Edwards leaned slightly forward. She'd barely touched her coffee since he'd poured for her, which made him wonder if she might prefer tea instead. He would have to ask. "Furthermore, the date proves it was recently written, which means his feelings for her have not wavered these past five years."

A valid point James had not yet considered. He did so now and was slowly reminded of Mr. Thompson's departure from Summervale. "She refused to leave her room when he left and remained there for days after, claiming malaise."

"Did you terminate his employment or—"

"No. He came to speak with me here, in my study. My father had recently passed away, so I was somewhat distracted by my new duties." That entire year had been a bit of a blur. He'd just graduated from University and was on his way home when his father had suffered what the physician claimed to have been too much strain on the heart. He'd been dead two days by the time James arrived to be swept up in funeral arrangements and the management of the estate. "I recall Mr. Thompson saying my sister had outgrown his teachings. He suggested getting her ready for her debut, even said such a thing might lift her spirits."

"Sounds to me like he was a considerate man, aware of his own limitations, who cared enough for your sister to separate himself from her in favor of giving her not what either of them might have wanted, but what he believed she needed."

"Perhaps." It certainly wasn't impossible. Another thought pushed its way to the forefront. "The nature of the note also suggests frequent correspondence, which means she never stopped caring for him."

"Which does imply that she wasn't in love with your friend, Harrington, or that she would have been looking forward to marrying him."

As Harrington had implied she had been.

Resting his elbow on the armrest, James brought his hand up to cover his mouth while trying to plot a path for himself. Failing to do so, he turned to Miss Edwards. "What do you propose I do?"

"Well, the problem is that, based on what we know so far, Harrington is the only one with a motive right now."

"I refuse to believe that."

"And yet the chance exists that he found out about Mr. Thompson and how Tatiana felt about him." Miss Edwards spoke without wavering. "Even if Harrington isn't in love with her, he might still have succumbed to a fit of jealousy upon learning that his future bride's heart belonged to another."

"Enough to kill her though?" It seemed absurd to James. Harrington had known Tatiana since she was a little girl. He couldn't possibly have done such an awful thing. Could he?

"Humans are possessive creatures, my lord."

"I can't argue with that." It wasn't unheard of for men to retaliate after discovering another had made use of their mistress – women who rarely inspired feelings of love.

"The way I see it," Miss Edwards continued, "there are three primary reasons for committing an act as vile as murder. They are money, passion, and the need to silence a witness. If Harrington did it, the act could have been brought on by a passionate response – a bout of rage, in other words."

"Your assessment is surprising." He hadn't meant to say that, but now the words were out, they hung between them, awaiting a response.

"Why?"

"Because of how devoid of emotion it is."

She smiled for the first time since entering the study. "That is why you sought my counsel, is it not? Because I have no ties to anyone here and may therefore consider them all with complete objectivity?"

"Of course. It is just curious to watch, especially when comparing my assessment of all that has happened and those potentially involved. Keeping emotion out of it, preventing myself from favoring one individual over another, is impossible."

Miss Edwards nodded. "That is understandable. You do not want the culprit to be one of your friends but rather a servant?"

He winced. "I would much prefer if it were a stranger."

She said nothing to this, and he understood additional comment was pointless. When she stood and smoothed her skirt, he stood as well. "I ought to get on with my work." She took a step back in the direction of the door.

James wished she didn't have to go. He wished they could sit and talk for the rest of the day without anyone troubling them. But she was right. She'd already stayed too long. If she didn't leave his study soon, Mrs. Fontaine would likely come looking for her, and being found here alone with him wasn't something he wanted to put Miss Edwards through.

"Let me know if you think of anything else," he said.

Her hand was already on the door handle. "I will."

To remind her he was there if she needed anything else, that his offer from earlier still stood, was tempting. He refrained only because he respected her far too much to pressure her any further. She'd rejected him, after all, and he would do well to abandon all hope of seduction, however loath he was to do so.

CHAPTER SEVEN

JANE'S LEGS SHOOK AS SHE walked away from the study. It had taken extreme focus for her to resist the Earl of Camden's advances. So she'd feigned affront and indignation, tossed his proposal back like an insult, and pretended she'd never consider such a thing, when nothing could be further from the truth. Because she'd been considering it since the moment she'd first laid eyes on him, not just in the flesh but as nothing more than a painted canvas hung on display.

But this was not the twenty-first century. Casual flings did not exist between men and women unless the woman in question was a whore, so the thing that had stopped her was not a need to protect her virtue, for that was lost long ago. Nor was it the concern she had about falling in love with him and then having to leave him behind if she found a way back to her own time. It was the notion that Camden had thought she would happily have an affair with him, that she was the sort of woman who'd welcome his proposition without caring one whit about what happened afterward.

Ironically, she might have been okay with it if

they hadn't been in Regency England. She might have treated herself to a one night stand with him as a means by which to get over her awful breakup with Geoffrey. Both would have been consenting adults with no expectations of the other. But that was not the case here, so she supposed it came down to perspective.

"Goodness gracious, Jane!" It was Mrs. Fontaine and she was hastening toward her. "I have looked everywhere for you without a sign to be found. Heaven's girl, where have you been?"

Jane straightened her spine and tilted her chin. "His lordship called for refreshments."

"Well!" Mrs. Fontaine's eyes were as sharp as a vulture's. She dipped her chin while carrying out a careful assessment of Jane's expression. "Lord Rockwell wishes to take a morning bath, so you'll have to help Margaret heat up the water. Mr. Goodard has carried several pails upstairs already."

"I'll get to it right away," Jane promised. She turned and marched toward the stairs and almost collided with Mr. Snypes who was rounding a corner.

He caught her swiftly by the elbow. "Careful, Jane." His eyes met hers and although they were kind, they also conveyed a tremendous amount of pain.

Straightening, Jane thanked him for his assistance. "Are you all right?"

His lips widened into a tight smile. "Of course. It was just a slight collision."

"That is not...I mean...Lady Tatiana's death and—"

"She did not deserve what happened to her."

He glanced away, cleared his throat, and stepped around Jane. "If you will excuse me."

Jane watched him go for a second while contemplating his reaction, then caught herself and proceeded to climb the stairs. She had a job to do after all, and getting thrown out because she failed to do it wasn't an option.

So she spent her time sweeping and dusting, changing bed sheets, mending clothes, polishing silver, and preparing baths. The latter chore was the only one that filled her with longing. Going for days on end without washing properly was not something she was accustomed to, but requesting a bath would be considered highly inappropriate. She had a pitcher and basin like the rest of the servants and a washcloth that went along with it. But it was a far cry from the comfort of a warm bath, which was probably what propelled Lord Rockwell to whisper close to her ear as she started to leave his room, "You are more than welcome to join me, Jane."

The thought of doing so did not agree with her at all. "Thank you, my lord, but I have other things to attend to."

"Like Camden, no doubt," he said with a chuckle.

Jane's cheeks heated, but rather than flee, she straightened her spine and stared Rockwell down. "Perhaps." What the hell was she doing, suggesting such a thing? All she knew was that she felt a need to put this arrogant aristocrat in his place.

But Rockwell didn't seem to care. If anything, he looked amused. "Then you had better be off." She'd almost reached the door when he added, "He deserves a lovely woman to ease his pain and offer some pleasure, so I hope you are up to the task."

With her heart pounding in her chest, Jane slipped out into the hallway and pressed her back to the wall while struggling for breath. Good lord! Rockwell certainly didn't lack the courage to speak his mind, did he? And she…Jane inhaled deeply and pushed away from the wall, aware her entire body trembled. All she could think of now was Camden and what Rockwell had said. *Ease his pain. Offer some pleasure.* She had the power to do precisely that, and damn it all if she didn't want to.

His face lingered in her mind's eye every second of every day. Her thoughts when she lay in bed at night invariably strayed to the wild imaginings of what it would be like if she only surrendered. And there was a pull – an undeniable pull that drew her to him in a way no other man had ever drawn her. It surpassed anything she'd ever felt with Geoffrey, and fighting it was proving to be a torturous affair.

But experience had taught her to think things through and avoid rash decisions based solely on sexual need. She had to be smart and consider the possibility that there was no going home. And what then? She had nowhere to go, no money, no family or friends beyond the people she knew here at Summervale. And they would all judge her if they discovered she'd slept with the master. Her reputation would be ruined.

With this in mind, she drew a lungful of air and made to return below stairs to the kitchen. But she didn't get far before Mr. Snypes appeared once more, this time blocking her path near the stairs. "We meet again," he said, coming toward her.

Jane slowed her progress until she stood immediately before him. "So we do."

He rocked back on his heels and nodded. "You should have known her."

The comment threw Jane momentarily off guard. "The earl's sister?"

"Lady Tatiana would have liked you."

"How can you possibly know that?"

He studied her for a moment. "Because you're likeable, Jane. Don't think I have not taken notice."

"You've been watching me?" The idea sent a chill down her spine, not because Mr. Snypes wasn't attractive or charming in his own sort of way, or because he'd given her any reason to fear him, but because of the loneliness that seemed to seep from his every pore.

A sad smile crept into place on his face. "It's not a crime, admiring a pretty woman." His hand suddenly rose to her cheek, his fingers brushing against her jaw.

"I believe that depends," Jane muttered. Her heart was in her throat. This wasn't normal. Having this man caress her like this without her offering any encouragement at all was wrong – a violation of her personal space and a reminder of her inferior position here.

Angered, she backed up a step and knit her brow, prepared to give him a piece of her mind. "Mr. Snypes! I—"

"You too, Jane?" He snorted and dropped his hand. "Am I so abhorrent that not even you, a mere maid, would take a fancy to me?"

"You forget yourself, sir."

His jaw clenched and for a second she feared he might shout at her. But then his face twisted and he turned away, leaving her there to wonder at what had transpired.

Camden. She needed to speak with him right away. Because what she'd just witnessed was not okay. It left her feeling rattled and uncertain. More than that, it made her wonder who else had rejected Mr. Snypes and why it had been so important for him to win a little affection from a woman he barely knew.

But when she drew closer to the library, the angry words resonating from within gave her pause. Approaching the door, she paused to listen. Only one man could be heard and that was Camden, his voice cutting the air like a blade demanding justice. Tempted to retreat, Jane hesitated a second. The matter she wished to discuss with him could wait until the following day. And yet, she sensed she was needed – that he required an anchor in the storm he was caught up in.

Her knock was quick, followed by instant silence, and then the command for her to enter. She did so slowly, almost fearing what she would find. Her gaze went directly to Camden whose hair was in disarray, a few stray locks falling over his brow in a wild way that made him look rather dangerous.

Jane's heartbeat quickened. She gave a hasty look in Harrington's direction and saw the viscount appeared to be in a state of shock. "Lord Camden." Her words came naturally, without any effort as she moved toward him. He did not move but stood as if frozen, his eyes dark with restrained fury as he stared across at his friend. "You must try to calm yourself."

His jaw tightened against the clenching of teeth.

"How can I when all the evidence I have collected suggests his involvement in Tatiana's death?"

Jane sucked in a breath while Harrington held up both hands in visible protest. While the earl had been alone, the idea of Harrington's possible involvement had apparently festered. Guilt squeezed at her heart. *She'd* made the suggestion while trying to understand all the facts they'd gathered so far. But that didn't mean they'd arrived at the right conclusion yet.

"I would never harm your sister, Camden. You have to believe me!"

"You did not love her though, did you? More than that, she was in love with someone else, which means that your assurance about her being excited to wed you, all that talk about her longing to make your engagement public, cannot have been true. Can it?"

Harrington stared back at Camden while Jane quietly watched. It hadn't occurred to her to warn the earl not to say anything about their findings until they had been confirmed. But it was too late for that now. His anguish had morphed into fury and clouded his judgment.

"I can explain," Harrington said. He sounded tired and defeated, his eyes gazing blankly into the void. And then he blinked, appeared to focus and gather himself. "You are right about Tatiana loving another. She confessed it to me the day before she died, but the man in question was not a possible match for her. He—"

"Used to be her tutor," Camden said.

Harrington nodded. "Our marriage would not have been a love match, but that does not mean I did not care for her. Her happiness mattered to me, Camden, which was why I promised to give her the freedom she wanted and allow her to maintain her connection with Mr. Thompson as long as she allowed me to pursue my own interests."

"Are you saying you were encouraging her to keep Mr. Thompson as her lover?" Jane had certainly heard of open marriages but had never known the subject to be aired quite so candidly.

Harrington nodded. "It was what she wanted."

"But…" Camden sounded thoroughly confused. He shook his head. "How could you have allowed that as her husband? How could you live like that without being bothered by it, regardless of whether you loved her or not?"

Harrington shrugged. "I am not selfish enough to insist upon holding her captive while I go philandering about as I please. It would not have been fair."

"So you admit to me, her brother, that you would have been unfaithful?" Camden's disbelief was evident in his tone.

"If that is what you wish to call it, then yes, Camden, that is precisely what I am admitting, though I do feel as though you are being shortsighted."

"Really?"

"Yes!" Harrington closed the distance between them and stared straight into his friend's angry gaze. "She could not marry Mr. Thompson, but with me she could have at least continued to enjoy the love he and she felt for each other while I offered friendship and protection."

Camden shook his head. "What of children? How would you have handled it if she had conceived a child by him?"

Harrington's gaze did not waver, though the edge of his mouth did twitch ever so slightly. And then, spontaneously, he reached up and cupped Camden's cheek with his hand. "I would have been incredibly grateful, and I would have loved him or her as my own."

Jane stood in stupefied silence, watching the troubled expression on Harrington's face and the heartbreaking depth of emotion brightening his eyes, until his hand fell away and he took a step back. It seemed to take immeasurable amounts of control for him to gather himself, yet he did, his composure returning gradually to the well-polished gentleman she knew him to be. Not a hint of longing remained, hidden beneath a now cool façade as he turned away and walked to the door.

Once there, he paused to address his friend. "I hope we can put this matter behind us now, Camden. As you have no doubt discovered —" he darted a look in Jane's direction "—our positions will often result in unhappiness. Your sister and I were merely attempting to find a workable solution."

"Do you believe him?" Camden asked once Harrington was gone.

"I do." Feeling a need to be near him, Jane moved a little closer to where he stood. "How long have you known him?"

Camden blinked and turned his head toward her. "Since the age of thirteen. We shared a room together at Eton."

"And in all of those years, it never occurred to you that he was in love with you?"

Camden's mouth dropped open, and for a long

moment after, she could see him trying to make sense of that. Eventually he shook his head. "What?"

"It was very evident in the way he spoke to you. The way he touched you and the way he—"

"No, Miss Edwards. You cannot possibly suggest such a thing. It is not right!"

Sympathizing, Jane reached for his hand. She knew his nineteenth-century views would not be as accepting of such a thing as hers were. "Why?" she pressed, because she felt it was important for him to know who his friend really was and the sacrifice he'd been willing to make for Camden and his sister. "Because he's a man?"

All he did was nod in response.

"And as a man, he must love a woman?"

"What you are suggesting goes against nature." His voice had gone unbearably quiet.

"No, my lord. What I am suggesting is that your friend's existence must be extraordinarily lonely. Imagine having to live with something like this in a world where being…different…is punishable by death?" She'd read about this as part of her research and knew that it would be another forty-three years before homosexuality only carried a prison sentence. "A man like him will never be free. Not in this lifetime. He will never know what it is to hold the one he loves in his arms or to marry that person before the eyes of God."

Tears welled in her eyes as she spoke, the sadness she felt on Harrington's behalf so excessive, she could not bear it. She placed a hand on Camden's arm and pressed down gently. "Have some compassion, my lord, and consider the offer he made to your sister. It was kind and deserves your appreciation. You cannot deny that."

He seemed to struggle with that for a moment, then he slowly raised his gaze to hers. "How can your view be so different from the norm?" He stared at her with inquisitive eyes. "It is as though you see a world I have yet to discover."

How was she to respond to that?

"Had you not been here," he added, before she could form an appropriate response, "I fear I would have lost control." His hand settled against her waist, and although she knew she should not allow such intimate contact, she lacked the strength to deny it. "I need you, Jane. I need you more than I have ever needed anyone else before."

The declaration coupled with the use of her first name left her feeling rather unbalanced. In fact, she could hardly breathe on account of the rapid beat of her pulse. It drummed swiftly beneath her skin, stirring her senses, and causing her nerves to collide in her belly. "My lord…" Dear God, if he kissed her, it would be her undoing.

"James." His hand shifted, pulling her closer, so close she could see the traces of gold in his eyes and the hint of stubble beginning to emerge along his upper lip. "I want you to call me James."

And before she could think, before she could form a plan of retreat, he dipped his head and pressed his mouth to hers, scattering all of her thoughts and making her mind go blank. The only thing that remained was acute awareness of how he felt and how her body responded. It was as if a burned-out furnace had been re-ignited, hotter than ever before, and although it might not have been wise and she might regret it later, she chose

THE GIRL WHO STEPPED INTO THE PAST

to live in the moment. Without hesitation, she wound her arms around his neck and threaded her fingers through the wisps of hair jutting over his jacket collar.

His hands pressed over her back in return, holding her to him with increased strength as he deepened the kiss with the same kind of urgency she was beginning to feel. It was an innate need to be as close to him as possible, to crawl beneath his skin, and cling to his very soul. It prompted her to run her hands over his shoulders, to grip his jacket, and wish they were somewhere else – somewhere infinitely more private and without the restraint of clothing.

"Christ, Jane." His voice licked the edge of her mouth, sending ripples of pleasure along her spine. Breaths fell in swift succession, just as heavily as hers, brushing over her skin before being replaced by his mouth.

All she could do was sigh as he kissed his way along the length of her neck while his hands tracked a similar path down over her waist and her hips. And then there was nothing between them, just the perfect fit of his hardness against her softness. Leaning back slightly while holding her firmly in place, he gazed down upon her with parted lips and half-lowered eyelids.

"You cannot imagine what you do to me, Jane."

Her cheeks heated with awareness. Desire was evident in his expression and in something else as well. "I can feel it," she confessed, provoking a low chuckle from deep within his chest.

"The things you say…" He kissed her again, more slowly than before.

Enjoying the languor, she moved her mouth in time to his, imparting all that she felt for this man and savoring the moment as if it might be her last.

When he pulled away a short while later, his eyes held a hint of gratitude and despair. "We should stop for now." He let her go, leaving her cold and alone. "At least until you have made up your mind."

"How so?"

He smiled then, like a boy about to cause mischief. "I want you, Jane. I want you so much I can barely see straight when I think of it, but I also refuse to form an attachment to a woman who will not be completely honest with me."

She stepped back swiftly, as if he'd slapped her. "First of all, you know I won't be your mistress."

"Then be my wife instead, Jane."

Had he really just offered marriage? Stunned, she shook her head. "That isn't possible, James, and even if it were, I don't know you well enough to consider such a permanent bond."

"So you will not be my mistress or my wife? Yet you permit me to kiss you as though you would happily be both?"

She could understand his anger and his confusion. His values were so very different from those she'd grown up with. "You do not love me, Camden, and even if you did, I am not the sort of woman a man like you could ever think of marrying."

Raising one hand, he raked his fingers roughly through his hair. "So this passion we share, this undeniable hunger we have for each other, means nothing to you?"

"It cannot. I refuse to allow it." Already she felt the sting of regret, the loss she knew was about to come.

His features hardened and his eyes grew distant. "You want to marry for love and will settle for nothing less." A grim bit of laughter was wrenched from his throat. "In truth, I have no choice but to admire your resolve, for it is stronger than mine. Where you are concerned, I am weak, ready to face the world's disapproval if only to have you in my bed every night for the rest of my life."

Jane shook her head in disbelief. "No. That is not weakness, James, it is folly. You are an earl, your father's heir. Responsibility and duty—"

"Hang responsibility and duty!"

"You cannot mean that." Jane forced herself to move away from him, aware that her heart was slowly being torn in two. She'd said what she'd felt was necessary in order to dissuade him, in order for her to have no regret or indecision when time came for her to leave. But rather than cast her aside, he'd offered her marriage.

Impossible.

And yet she could not help but consider it now, except she feared his sudden decision to make a scandalous choice for his future was born from the wrong reasons. All things considered, she suspected it had everything to do with physical attraction and hormones and very little to do with any developing form of affection.

In light of what she'd left behind, her break from Geoffrey and the knowledge that he had cared more about restricting her to a box she did not fit into than he had about her, made her want to ensure she made the right choice for herself where James was concerned. Because in the end, wanting to wrap her arms around a man and kiss him senseless wasn't enough. More was required if the relationship was to last—a point for her to keep in mind in the early nineteenth century where marriage was for life and divorce a thing of fiction.

And that was provided she stayed – provided she chose to give up the life she'd always known for a man she'd met just a few days ago. She almost laughed at the preposterousness of it.

Overwhelmed, she dropped into the nearest chair and placed her head in her hands. She had to try and think clearly on this. She had to—

"Will you share your concerns with me?"

His voice was close, and she realized he'd lowered himself to his haunches, his face now level with hers.

"My concerns…" She shook her head. How on earth could she ever explain when her world had been flipped upside down and her mind was an absolute mess?

"You are clearly distressed." His hand settled lightly upon her knee. "Confide in me, Jane. Allow me to help."

Lowering her hands, she met his anxious gaze. "I wish I could but I can't. You would never believe what I tell you, and your ensuing distrust of me would be crippling."

Tilting his head, he seemed to consider that for a moment before eventually saying, "And yet it is your distrust of me that keeps you from opening up. How do you suppose I feel about that?" When she failed to answer, he asked a different question. "Do you still have feelings for this fiancé of yours? The one you ran away from? Is that what prevents you from accepting my offer?"

"No. No, it is nothing like that."

"What then? Your past or…" He swallowed, tightened his grip on her knee. "I would not judge you harshly if you were to tell me your innocence has been compromised."

Steeling herself, Jane nodded. "That is part of it."

He had the decency not to look the least bit horrified by this admission, which must have come as a blow. "What else is there?" he asked.

To tell him the truth was unwise. Jane knew this instinctively. It did not take a genius to discern what the consequence might be if she did so, and yet the insistence with which he looked at her compelled her to be honest at last. "Promise me that whatever your thoughts on what I'm about to tell you, you won't throw me out. Promise me you'll let me stay no matter what your opinion of me might be from this moment onward."

"Calm yourself, Jane. I promise to do what I can to help you with whatever problem you are facing." He brushed a lock of hair from her forehead with the gentlest stroke of his fingers. "It must be dire indeed to invoke such fear in your voice. Your entire body is trembling."

She licked her lips and tried to ignore the pounding of her heart. "You know how you think I'm different from any other woman you've ever met?" When he nodded she said, "Well, that's because I am."

"In what sense?"

It took every effort to force the next few words from her mouth. "I'm not from here, James. Not just from England but from this time."

Incomprehension marred his features. "What does that mean?"

"I'll tell you, but you'll have to keep an open mind."

"I will do my best," he promised.

"Know that I am just as stunned by what has happened to me as you will be to hear of it. Indeed, it defies all logic and comprehension, but the fact of the matter is that I was born on March 1, 1990, almost two hundred years from now."

James blinked and a rapid half laugh escaped him. "You cannot be serious. You cannot honestly think I would believe such a thing might be possible? I mean…" He stood and stepped away from her. "All I wanted from you was honesty, and instead you come up with this fabrication, this utter nonsense?"

She stood as well. "Why do you think I kept it from you?" When he retreated another step, she advanced. "Because I knew this would be your reaction. But consider what you know. Think of the suddenness with which I arrived here, of the way I was dressed, the way I speak, and the things I know or…don't know."

His hesitance was obvious. "I feel as though you are trying to make a fool of me, Jane. What you are suggesting is utterly impossible."

"Of course it is, yet here I am." Emotion crept into her voice. "Do you think this is what I wanted? That I'm enjoying this?" Her eyes began to sting as desperation took hold. "It's not as if I can simply board the next ship back to New York. Going home is not that easy for me."

He studied her while she silently willed him to

believe her.

Eventually he shook his head. "You must have hit your head or…suffered an attack of some sort. Perhaps I should send for my physician and have him take a look at you."

Jane squeezed her eyes shut to stop the tears that threatened from falling. "No," she murmured. "That won't be necessary. I'm quite all right."

"I seriously doubt that. Especially not if you actually believe what you have just told me is true."

Opening her eyes, she saw the sympathy etched upon his brow in the form of a frown. Her lips quivered ever so slightly. Telling him the truth had obviously been a mistake. He thought her delusional, which was probably what her opinion of him would have been if he'd arrived on the balcony of her New York apartment and told her he'd come from the nineteenth century.

His reaction right now was normal, but after what they'd just shared and the bond she'd felt forming between them, it made her feel more alone than she had before she'd confided her secret. It was as if a hole had opened inside her, swallowing up all hope and leaving her drained.

Drawing a fortifying breath, she decided to push aside her despair and focus on helping him instead. A change of subject was certainly welcome, so she said, "I came across Mr. Snypes on my way down here. He said the most curious thing." She then described the strange encounter, adding that he'd behaved as though a recent rejection had pained him. "If your sister was the subject of his affection and she dismissed his advances then—"

"Snypes was with me the evening my sister was

killed. He and I were discussing a potential business investment when we heard Tatiana scream."

Jane tried to envision the events as they must have happened to the best of her ability. "How long had the two of you been talking before then?"

"For about ten minutes or so."

"And what about the rain?"

His frown deepened. "What do you mean?"

She was following a train of thought that might not lead anywhere, but if she'd learned anything from all the detective shows she'd watched, it was the importance of facts. "Had it been raining for long or had the downpour just started at the time when you heard the scream?"

"I do not recall. I…I think it came on suddenly."

Jane nodded. "So then, Mr. Snypes could still have committed the crime before the two of you sat down together to discuss your business investment."

"No." He shook his head. "As I said, he was with me when Tatiana screamed."

"Except we have to consider the possibility that the scream you heard wasn't Tatiana's." Jane watched as James's eyes widened. "What if it was someone else'?"

A nearby clock ticked away the seconds while she waited for him to respond. Eventually he said, "I suppose that is possible. But then why would they not have come forward?"

"There are those who do not wish to get involved with something like this. Especially if they don't feel as though they are able to help in any way."

"But if it was a maid who screamed, perhaps upon seeing Tatiana on the terrace, then there could be a gap in the timeline there – a series of minutes between the murder and the scream – during which it would have been possible for Snypes to commit the crime. Even though I am loath to believe him capable of such a thing."

"I understand. It is just that we have to consider all angles." She held his gaze. "There's also your butler, Hendricks, the grooms, your footmen, your valet, and then of course Rockwell."

"I have known them all for years. My servants are loyal and Rockwell is my friend."

"So is Harrington, yet you did not know the most important thing about him."

James groaned and thrust a hand through his hair. "How am I to face him now? The thought of discussing eligible young ladies and marriage prospects with him from this point onward seems absurd."

"I think the most important thing to remember is that he's your friend and that it's your duty to keep his secret." She smiled a little. "Besides, he doesn't know that you know this. Perhaps pretending you don't will be the easiest way forward for both of you."

"You might be right." James took a deep breath and released it while shoving his hands into his trouser pockets. "Thank you for advising me. For helping me with all of this. I hope you can forgive my inability to believe what you have told me about yourself."

She chuckled slightly. "I wouldn't have believed it either if I were in your position. To me, however, it's reality. It's the reason why I'm wary of getting involved with you."

Before he could say anything in response to that, his mother entered the room. Her expression was hard, her eyes assessing as she looked from one to the other.

"What is going on here?" she asked, her voice rattling what remained of Jane's composure. When Lady Camden narrowed her gaze on her, she took an instinctive step back. "Is my son keeping you from your chores, Jane?"

"No, my lady." Jane bobbed a curtsey that earned a frown from the dowager countess. "He merely—" The frown deepened, cutting her off. Flustered, she muttered a quick, "Excuse me," then headed for the door and disappeared into the hallway beyond, leaving James to deal with the most unnerving woman Jane had ever had the displeasure of knowing.

CHAPTER EIGHT

"**Y**OU FRIGHTENED HER, MAMA."

His mother showed no hint of remorse. "I have asked Rockwell if he will invite his youngest sister to join us," she said, ignoring his comment.

James stared. "Lady Elise? But she is no more than sixteen years of age!"

"All the more reason for you and her to become better acquainted with each other before she debuts next Season."

"Mama." The horror of what she suggested came crashing down over his head. "You cannot be serious."

"She is a respectable match, and since you have thus far wasted all other opportunities to get yourself settled, I have taken it upon myself to get the job done for you." She tipped her chin up. "An heir to the title must be secured and…with your sister's passing, my chance of having grandchildren has been severely diminished."

James blinked. "This is the first time I have ever heard you mention a desire for grandchildren. All you have ever done is push Tatiana and me at every potential partner there was." His poor sister had probably grown so exasperated by it, she'd eventually chosen to settle for Harrington.

"You are my children. Ensuring your future was always of great importance to me."

"Even at the cost of our happiness?" When she gave him a quizzical look, he said, "I will never consider Lady Elise, Mama."

"Why?"

Because I want Jane.

His mother's eyes widened as if she had heard him. Her upper lip curled with disgust. "You fancy the maid!" Her hands clenched into fists at her sides. "Then have her, you fool. Take her and get her out of your system before Lady Elise arrives here."

"It is not so simple, Mama." James did his best to keep his voice level, to prevent himself from lashing out in response to his mother's crass suggestion. "Miss Edwards deserves better." Even if her explanation regarding her presence at Summervale was completely absurd. He still cared for her, still longed for her, still hoped to find a way for her to be his.

His mother scoffed. "She deserves what is fitting for her station, which will never be more than a possible tryst with you."

"Mama." He ground the word out between his teeth. "Miss Edwards is a good natured woman."

"So were the maids your father enjoyed during the course of our marriage." The bitterness with which she spoke was palpable. "They were all so clever, so kind, so sweet, so deserving of his attention while I...I was the woman who got in the way, the one who always complained about having to share her husband."

James's heart thudded against his chest. He wasn't prepared for such a confession or for the tears that spilled down his mother's cheeks in the seconds that followed. Without thinking, he closed the distance between them and wrapped his arms around her slender figure. "I never knew," he murmured against the top of her head while she sobbed into his shoulder.

"You were just a boy, off chasing rabbits or digging trenches most of the time." She pulled back and he released her. "Besides, I believe your father did his best to keep you and your sister in the dark. Your opinion of him mattered, you see, far more than mine ever did."

"I am sorry, Mama. It cannot have been easy for you to live like that."

With a sigh, she sank down onto a chair. "I loved him, James. That was what made it so horribly awful, discovering he didn't feel the same about me."

"So then, if this has been your experience, why would you not want me to find the happiness you lacked? With Lady Elise I shall be miserable, of that I assure you."

"Perhaps, but what other option is there? You know you cannot have Jane."

"Only because tradition and social etiquette say so. But there is no law preventing me from marrying whomever I choose, even if the woman in question does happen to be a maid."

His mother did not look convinced, but she didn't seem nearly as hostile toward the idea as she had five minutes earlier. "I cannot support you in this."

"You do not have to. If this is the course I choose, I will do so alone."

"The scandal will be immense."

He snorted and claimed the seat opposite hers. "Scandal is only something to fear if it threatens your happiness. Whether or not people judge me for turning my back on convention matters little to me as long as I have the right person by my side."

A weak smile formed upon his mother's lips. "I wish I had been as strong as you."

"Your choices were always different because of your sex."

"I suppose that is true." She dabbed at the last remaining tears still clinging to her lashes. "Do you ever wonder if things might change?"

"I do not know." His thoughts strayed to Jane as he spoke. He'd betrayed her trust in him when she'd finally chosen to do as he asked and confided the truth, or at least her version of it. But for him to believe her was difficult. It went against his every instinct, and yet, deep inside, he trusted her more than anyone else he'd ever known.

Which was why he found himself outside her bedchamber door that very same evening.

Raising his hand, he gave a quick knock. The door opened a moment later, revealing the woman whose mouth had been pressed against his in a passionate kiss just a few hours earlier. Until he'd ruined it all by dismissing her story.

"Do you mind if I come in?"

Jane stared at James in dismay. "You want to meet

with me in my bedroom?" Was the man insane? "You can't be serious. I mean, you know what everyone else will think if we're found out."

"No one needs to know. Not as long as you grant me entry quickly so I can get out of this hallway."

Against her better judgment, she relented and opened the door wide enough for him to come in. He closed it swiftly behind him, locking it for good measure. "What you told me earlier, about arriving here from the future…I want to believe you, but it is a struggle for me to do so. Perhaps if you could tell me more about the place you have come from or some other details to help me understand, it might help."

"You want me to prove it to you." Although a small part deep inside her heart wished it wasn't necessary for her to do so, she wasn't surprised. So she went to the bed and lifted the mattress to pull out the dress, underwear and flats she'd been wearing the day she'd arrived. "I hid these so no one would find them." She placed the bundle on top of the bed and unfolded the dress first. "Look here," she said, showing him the designer tag and care label.

He squinted down at it. "100% cotton." He looked up for a second before returning his attention to the label. "Machine wash warm."

"That means this dress can be loaded into an electric washing machine with detergent and washed in warm water. A motor makes the barrel spin round and round while water is added. There's no manual labor involved at all."

"Are you able to draw this device for me?"

"Of course." She went to the desk in her room

and pulled out paper and pencil. "It is square, like this, with a round glass door on the front and buttons in the upper right hand corner." She produced a quick sketch. "There are different models, of course, but this is what mine looks like."

"You had your own?"

She nodded. "Most people do."

An awkward bit of silence fell between them while he continued to stare down at her rough illustration of a washing machine. "Can you draw something else from this future of yours?"

Grinning, she set the pencil to paper once more. It didn't take long for her to sketch out a car, a TV, an airplane and a laptop. "People rarely send letters by mail anymore. They use a computer which has a keyboard for typing and a screen that can display an endless number of images. If you want to learn something new, you just type your question into it and it immediately gives you the answer."

"I find it hard to envision."

"It is the sort of thing you have to see, just like the rest of these things are. I mean, I don't suppose you're having an easier time of imagining people climbing into a metal tube that then takes flight and carries them across the world."

He laughed at that. "No. Not really."

"Well, it took me about seven hours to travel from New York to England like that and…" She paused while he adjusted his brain to this information. "There are even people in space these days."

"What?"

"We've been to the moon," she explained.

That seemed to be the last drop in an already overflowing glass of water. James gaped at her as if she were mad. "How can that be?"

"Technology developed at an increasingly rapid rate during the twentieth century. I'm always impressed whenever I think of it." She watched while James placed his fingertips at his temples as if he felt a headache coming on. "I can offer further proof if you need it." She went to the bed and picked up her bra. "Have you ever seen an item of clothing like this?"

He stared at the lacy item as if it glowed. "No, but it does not take much imagination to know what it is for."

She rolled her eyes and smiled at his boyishness. "Stays and corsets are a thing of the past. What you'll want to notice with this item, however, is not so much its construct, but rather the fabric from which it is made." Pulling out the tag, Jane handed the item over to James so he could read it.

"Nylon, lycra, polyester…I have never heard of these materials before."

"Because they have not yet been invented. They're all man made."

"But how?" His expression was one of dismay.

Jane shrugged. "I'm not entirely sure, to be honest, and it's no longer something I'm able to look up."

Handing the bra back to her, James lowered himself onto a wooden chair and just sat there for a moment, staring out at the room as a whole. "I hardly know what to say."

"It's a lot to take in all at once, I'm aware of that." She returned her clothes to their hiding spot. "Do you think you might believe me though?"

He gradually nodded. "Yes. I think I might."

She breathed a sigh of relief. "Thank God." Her entire body quivered with relief. "I don't know what I would have done otherwise. Especially not if I end up having to stay here. The thought of it…"

"Then you would choose to return if the chance to do so arose?" He watched her cautiously, assessingly.

"Yes. I believe I would." Yet even as she said it, she wondered if doing so would be a mistake. "What sort of life can I possibly have here, James?"

"A good one, I suspect, if you would agree to be my wife." Hope brightened his eyes and drew her to him.

"The age you live in is not as liberal as mine." When he frowned, she explained, "You have to marry a lady of your own social standing. Doing otherwise would be ruinous to your reputation."

"My mother said the same thing, but what if I choose to thwart social expectations in favor of seeking happiness instead? My wealth is stable enough, my investments secure. Whether or not the rest of the peerage shuns me will hardly affect my comfort or yours."

She stared at him in amazement, then lowered herself to the bed. "But you hardly know me! I have been here only five days!"

"Is that really all?" He looked genuinely surprised. "It seems like so much longer." When she failed to respond, he grasped her hands between his own and told her quietly, "I have met countless eligible young ladies over the years. I have danced and conversed with them, and I have felt nothing. Until you came along and proved to me that they were not the women my heart or my soul were seeking. You are, Jane. You, with your impossible story and outspoken candor." He reached for her and squeezed her hands ever so slightly. "You have turned my world upside down, prompted me to consider a future I never would have considered before, encouraged me to hope for a measure of happiness I never believed would be mine."

"James—"

"I know you have reservations. I know you have no desire to be here and that you will leave if doing so becomes possible, but I cannot shake the feeling that fate has brought you to me and that our paths were destined to cross." He flattened his lips before adding, "What we make of this unlikeliness is up to us."

It was hard for Jane to find the right words, so she remained silent for a long moment after. He'd offered marriage, though he could not possibly know what that would entail with an independent-minded woman such as herself. She would balk at any limitations he or society wanted to place on her. Her opinions on various issues would likely cause a great deal of trouble as well, especially since she was not the sort who'd be able to keep such thoughts to herself.

And then of course there was the convenience of living in the time in which she'd grown up. She might get used to doing without a TV or the internet or even a car, but a proper toilet, not to mention toilet paper, toothpaste, deodorant, and tampons would all be sorely missed if she stayed any longer than she already had.

Still, she had to accept the possibility of being

permanently stuck here. In which case, James's proposal was the most tempting one going forward. Especially since she was already falling for him harder than she ever had for Geoffrey. How such a thing could be when she'd known Geoffrey for three years and spent the last year living with him was amazing. But there it was, a piece of reality thrust in her face. With James there was something more – a connection that reached to her core and anchored her firmly to him. It filled her heart to overflowing and fed her soul with immeasurable joy. Whether or not it would turn into love remained to be seen, but she sensed it was only a matter of time before it happened.

"This notion that we are fated to be together," she said while weaving her way through her muddled thoughts, "I feel it too."

"I know you do. I can see it in your eyes whenever you look at me."

"But I am torn," she explained, determined to be as honest with him as she could be. "I want a future with you, but I also want to return to my time."

"You fear you might miss your friends and family? That they will worry over your disappearance?"

It was a logical assumption, but it was wrong. "I am an only child, as were my parents, and they both died about three years ago in a car accident." It had been the worst moment of her life when the cops had arrived on her doorstep to deliver the news. She still relived it now and again in her nightmares. "Another car ran a red light – a traffic signal that tells other cars to stop – and…my dad reportedly died on the spot, but my mom got to suffer a few days in the hospital before her body gave up."

"I am so very sorry to hear that, Jane."

"As for friends," she said, quickly changing the subject, "There are some, but none I would pick if it meant losing you. What I fear I might miss the most is the way of life, the conveniences, my job as a writer. I cannot be the sort of wife who sits around doing needlework or painting or spends her time managing a household. I have no accomplishments, and I do not ride either."

He smiled at that. "I could teach you how to if you wished to learn, but I would never insist you do so. Neither would I insist you be a traditional nineteenth-century wife when much of your allure is in your uniqueness. I love how different you are, the way you speak your own mind, and your willingness to apply yourself to whatever task is required of you."

"Like being a maid while trying to solve a murder."

"Exactly." He pulled her to him until she was forced to exchange her seat for his lap. "You challenge me, Jane. You broaden my horizons and make me question the world I live in. And if you want to continue writing, of course you can do so. For me, the most important thing is to have you by my side, as my partner."

"Would you be willing to discuss your investments and finances with me?" she asked, because if he would, then that would truly prove his devotion since Regency women weren't usually privy to their husband's affairs.

"As a matter of fact, I have a new investment in mind and would love to hear your opinion on it."

His hand rose to her chin, tilting it slightly so he could lean forward and press his mouth gently to hers. It was a slow kiss, a loving kiss, the sort that made her feel rather lightheaded and dizzy.

When his lips parted, she mirrored the movement, allowing him to deepen the kiss on a murmur that made her heart tremble. She ran her hand through his hair, loving the feel of it spilling across her fingers. His hand flattened securely against her back, holding her in place. He tasted sweet and slightly fruity, like rich chocolate accompanied by wine. The caress was slow, measured, and oh so perfect. It warmed her insides, the way tea drunk by an open fire would, or a hot leisurely bath on a frosty afternoon might do.

"Imagine doing this for the rest of your life, Jane," he whispered close to her ear.

"You tempt me too easily, James." Her lips touched the side of his neck to provoke a sigh of pleasure. His hand fell to her thigh, and the warmth inside her became a blaze. She wanted this man, wanted him with every fiber of her being, and he clearly wanted her too.

In that instant, she made a decision. Because what if she did return to her own time and lost him? The regret she would feel at not knowing what it might be like to be intimate with him would haunt her forever. Loss would be hers, but she could at least have something more than a kiss to carry her through it.

So she pushed at him gently and slid off his lap. His lips parted in protest, his eyes clouding with a mixture of longing and confusion.

Without uttering a word, she toed off her shoes,

removed her stockings and undid the ties securing her gown at her side. The fabric slipped, revealing the stays and chemise she wore underneath.

James stared, his hands curling into fists. "Jane…"

She pulled her arms free from the sleeves and allowed the garment to fall. With racing heartbeats, she then untied her stays, tossed aside the garment, and drew a deep breath. Her entire body trembled as she pulled the chemise up over her head, leaving her body entirely bare.

Slowly, James stood. "You are even more glorious than I imagined you would be."

Heat scorched her cheeks. "You wondered how I would look without any clothes?"

He caught her waist and drew her flush against his much harder body. "Of course," he murmured, so low and seductive a shiver scurried across her shoulders. "I have lain awake every night since your arrival, wondering what it would be like to have you in my bed."

Her breaths grew increasingly ragged, more so when he showed her how capable he was of tending to her needs. Slowly, he caressed every curve, covering her in kisses until she grew restless. His touch was perfect, skimming across her skin with feather-soft lightness and making her want in a way she had never wanted before.

As soon as he'd shucked his clothing as well, she returned the favor. Torturing him in a similar way, she explored his body until he was equally mindless and desperate for more.

"You are everything I've ever dreamed of," he murmured. With trembling fingers, he pressed her hand over his heart and kissed her again. Long and deep and with all the certainty in the world.

"Please," she begged as she settled herself on the bed. "I need you, James." She reached for him, and he was instantly there, sinking into her warmth. Words of endearment followed and then he was loving her with his body while she clung to him and the promise he'd made.

"Yes," he murmured when she followed his rhythm and then, "yes" again as desire erupted around her. His mouth met hers, hard and possessive while waves of euphoria pulsed through her veins. And then he shuddered against her, swept away on the same burst of energy she had experienced seconds before.

"My God," he muttered as he collapsed on the bed beside her.

Breathing hard, he pulled her close and gathered her up in his arms, securing her tightly against his chest. With reverent tenderness, he touched his lips to her brow, telling her without the use of words the truth that was in his heart. "You dazzle me, Jane." His voice was soft. "I never imagined lovemaking could be so profound. It feels as though you reached inside me and touched my soul."

"I feel the same way," she told him softly. The experience had been soul-shattering. It would make it even harder for her to leave, but she would not let herself regret it. Not for a second.

His hand stroked over her hair, and his breathing settled into a calmer rhythm.

Needing to clear her mind of the conflicting hopes and dreams crashing through her, she tried to engage him in a conversation that wasn't about them. "So what's this new investment you mentioned earlier?"

He shifted slightly and stretched out his legs. "Snypes has a friend whose cousin plans on opening a factory in Birmingham. The grocer's shop he has been running for the past few years has proven to be quite successful, especially with regard to selling cocoa and drinking chocolate. That is the part of the business he now intends on expanding, and with the positive reviews he has been receiving, I am thinking of buying into it."

"Chocolate certainly is a desirable commodity." Jane rose up onto one elbow so she could gaze down at the man she had grown so incredibly fond of. "What is the name of the business? Perhaps I have heard of it?"

"Cadbury Tea Dealer."

Jane almost laughed. "Well, it won't continue dealing in tea for long." When he frowned, she told him seriously, "You ought to invest as much as possible in that company, James. Cadbury's will become one of the largest chocolate companies in the world. You and your descendants will make a fortune off of it."

"I hope they will be your descendants as well," he said with a gleam of mischief in his eyes. His hand found the curve of her bottom and squeezed.

Unable to bear the tug of war playing out within her, she chose to ignore it. Instead, she swung her leg across his thighs and rose onto her knees, straddling him while enjoying the thrill of the raw desire capturing his features.

"Your experience is clearly quite vast."

She stilled for a second, her pulse racing and her own need for closer contact with him thrumming through her. "Does that bother you?"

He snorted. "Not at all. Not as long as I am the man you choose above all others."

Lowering her head, she kissed him with all the tenderness she possessed. He was marvelous, the Earl of Camden, and she'd be a fool not to let him have what he wanted. Because in the end, it was what she wanted as well – a love so strong it bridged the fabric of time, uniting them and providing them with a chance to spend the rest of their lives together.

She thought of this as she moved with him against the bed sheets, offering herself and taking in equal measure until it felt as though she was riding across the sun. "James," she sighed as rapture shook her and sent her tumbling over the edge.

"Be mine," he said as he hugged her to him and kissed her cheek.

She chose not to answer for fear of ruining the moment, her brain warring with two contradictory responses. The first was, "Yes." The second, "I can't."

CHAPTER NINE

THE FOLLOWING DAY PASSED IN a bit of a blur. Focusing on her chores was impossible for Jane in the wake of the previous evening's events. She'd done what she'd told herself she could not do. She'd slept with him, which made her wonder a bit about what to do next. Because she really didn't want the rest of the servants finding out, or anyone else for that matter. Especially since she wasn't sure which foot to stand on at the moment.

After falling asleep in James's embrace, she'd awoken to fine him gone. He'd given her no indication of how to proceed from this point forward, so she could only assume she was to continue as maid until she accepted or refused his offer of marriage. The whole business left her with a sense of deflation she could not shake, but on the other hand, he probably felt no better having to deal with a woman who could not make up her mind about what she wanted.

Obviously, the biggest problem was that she wanted it all. In a perfect world she would take him with her back to her own time, except as far as

meddling with the fabric of time, that would probably take the cake. So then, in order to have him,
she would have to stay here, which was something
she was starting to think about more seriously now.
Especially if he accepted the woman she was with
no demand for her to change in any way. And who
was to say she couldn't make a success of things here
in Regency England? Perhaps she'd stand more of
a chance of becoming a successful romance author
during this time period. The genre was certainly
less competitive, so if she could only write in a way
that appealed to this day and age, she was confident
her novels would become popular.

Presently, however, she had more important
things to consider. Tatiana's murder remained
unsolved, and with James's mention of Rockwell's
sister arriving soon, there was much for her to do
besides finding the guilty culprit. She'd felt a flare
of jealousy upon hearing about Lady Elise, but
James had assured her she need not worry about
her.

"My mother invited her during a momentary
lapse in judgment and without consulting me. If it
were not rude, I would send the girl away again the
instant she gets here," he'd told her. "I expect her to
be thoroughly bored during her stay what with no
other ladies of her own age about."

Helping Margaret prepare another guest bedroom, Jane forced herself to think of everything
she and James had concluded so far. The last thing
they'd theorized, was the possibility that the scream
James had heard on the night of the murder had
not been Tatiana's. Jane caught the other end of the
bed sheet and pulled it tight around the corners of

the mattress.

"I was wondering…" She smoothed the sheet with the palm of her hand. "Where were you that night when Lady Tatiana was killed?"

Margaret froze. "I was in her bedchamber actually, returning a bit of mending to the dresser."

"So you heard her scream then?"

"I heard someone scream, but I don't believe it was her ladyship."

"Why not?"

Margaret grimaced and turned away to busy herself with a bit of dusting. "You're very curious about this whole thing."

"I'm trying to solve it," Jane confessed.

"Really?" Having turned toward her, Margaret stared at Jane with wide eyes.

Jane nodded. "Whoever did this has to be found and punished. So if you know something that you've not yet mentioned…"

"I'd say it was either Betsy or Tilly who screamed." Margaret bit her lip before adding. "It was high pitched. Cook and Mrs. Fontaine would have sounded different."

And since Betsy had been killed, the only person Jane could ask was Tilly.

She found her in the kitchen later that day, furiously scrubbing away at a pot, and was reminded of the tragic look in her eyes when Jane had first met her. At the time, she'd supposed the girl was simply distressed by what had transpired, but perhaps it was more than that. Perhaps she'd actually seen something.

"Can I talk to you for a second in private?" Jane asked as she sidled up next to Tilly. Soap suds frothed in the pot, covering Tilly's hands and arms all the way to her elbows.

"I'm a touch busy at the moment. Don't you see?"

"I do, but this will only take a moment, and it would be really helpful."

Glancing over her shoulder at Cook, Tilly set the pot aside with a sigh and wiped her hands on her apron. "I'm going to fetch some more water," she said and then led the way through to a door. It opened onto some steps leading up to a court-yard. "What is it then?" Tilly asked once they were alone. She reached for a bucket and set it beneath the pump.

"Were you near the terrace on the night when Lady Tatiana was killed?" Jane asked.

Color drained from Tilly's face. "Why do you ask?"

"Because someone screamed, and I'm trying to figure out who it was and if that person might have seen something."

"I didn't see anything other than the body." Her eyebrows had pulled together while the corners of her lips dipped downward.

"Why didn't you call someone?"

Tears welled in Tilly's eyes. "Because I wasn't supposed to be upstairs. It's not my place, but I realized the mints I'd made that afternoon might have been contaminated and—"

"What on earth do you mean?"

"It wasn't my fault. I mean, it was, I suppose, but it was an accident, Jane, you've got to believe me! And then I saw her ladyship, and I feared I might have had something to do with her death, so I ran and hid in my room."

Dumbfounded, it took a second for this new bit of information to seep in. "I take it these mints are sweets for his lordship's family and guests?"

Tilly nodded. "Cook usually makes them but she had an errand to run that day, so she left me to it after a bit of instruction." She gulped and swiped at her eyes. "It wasn't until she returned that I realized the egg I'd used wasn't from the new batch brought in that morning but from one she'd been meaning to throw out because it was old."

"And you were afraid of admitting to your mistake. Of what the consequence might have been?"

"First chance I got I snuck upstairs to remove the mints and replace them with fresh ones and…that's when I saw her."

"So you instinctively screamed and then ran so you wouldn't be discovered."

"Just so," Tilly confirmed. She wrung her hands on her apron. "Please don't tell anyone, Jane."

Unable to make such an assurance, Jane told her instead, "I've never heard of someone dying because they ate an old egg."

"I know, you're right, but I panicked. And then later on when I came to my senses, it was too late."

Jane nodded. "You did the right thing to confide this information now. It will help create a better picture of what happened that evening and increase the chance of finding her ladyship's killer."

"I hope so. Truly I do."

Jane gave a polite smile and then helped Tilly pump the water and carry the bucket back into the kitchen. From there, she took the servants stairs toward the main floor with the intention of giving the library a thorough dusting. But as luck would have it, Lady Camden was approaching from the right at the exact same moment Jane stepped out into the hallway. Naturally, fleeing was out of the question, unless Jane wanted to look like an absolute coward, which she didn't. So she dropped her gaze instead and bobbed a curtsey.

"Jane." The countess's voice was as dry as bark on a hot summer's day. "It has come to my attention that my son has developed something of a tendre for you."

Straight to the point then. Jane chose to deny it. "I don't know what you're talking about, my lady."

"Hmm…" The countess reached out and used one long pointy finger to tip Jane's chin up. Squinting, she peered into her upturned face. "I find that highly unlikely." Dropping her finger, she straightened her spine and looked down her nose at Jane. "You will of course dissuade such nonsensical affection and remind him of his duties."

"And why on earth would I do that?"

"Because your employment here depends on it, my dear." The countess leaned forward. "Do not make the error of supposing my son is the only one wielding power around here. If I want you gone, you shall disappear quickly enough. But for some reason, I suspect you are rather comfortable with your position and loath for it to change. Perhaps you need the funds, perhaps there is something else, but it is no matter. The point is, you will leave my son alone so he can give his attention to a woman who is deserving."

It took all the self-restraint Jane possessed and the biting of her tongue not to give the woman a sharp rejoinder. But after what she'd just been told, she held back the retort, allowing only a silent curse. "As you wish," she muttered. What did it matter anyway? It wasn't as if she loved James or he loved her. His only motive for offering marriage was so he could bed her as often as he chose, and her only motive to accept was so she wouldn't be viewed as a whore. If she stayed. Which she was really not sure she would.

"Good." The countess smiled. "Then we are in agreement."

Jane watched her saunter off while wondering how a woman like her could ever have mothered a son as kind and thoughtful as James. It just went to show that one could never judge a person based on their parents. With a groan, she continued toward the library, halting the moment she opened the door. It appeared as though the room was in utter chaos. Books had been pulled off shelves, opened up, and spread out on tables. And in the middle of all the clutter stood one man, his hunched over frame and frantic movements suggesting a state of absolute panic.

"Mr. Snypes?"

He seemed oblivious to her presence, deaf to her voice, so she went to him slowly and placed one hand on his arm. Flinching, he looked up instantly from the book he was holding, a wild expression widening his eyes and darkening his pupils. "Jane."

"What are you doing?" When he seemed confused, she allowed her gaze to shift to the room at large, waiting for him to follow her line of vision.

He did so shortly. "I…I…His lordship has not yet woken, so I thought I would try to find the letter."

Jane frowned. "What letter?"

As if not hearing her, he dropped the book and went to pick up another. "It has to be here somewhere."

"Mr. Snypes." She attempted to force her most authoritative tone – the one she recalled her French teacher using when she was in high school. "Will you please tell me what is going on?"

He looked up again as if startled. Uncertainty marred his features for a long, drawn out second until his forehead suddenly scrunched, and his lips drew tight, giving way to a look of extreme annoyance. "None of your business." He marched toward her and held the book out for her to take. The moment she took it, he clasped his hands behind his back. "I was looking for something on his lordship's behalf, but it seems as though it is not here." Waving a dismissive hand, he then said, "Now tidy this up, Jane. That is after all your job, is it not?"

"No. It bloody well isn't," she was tempted to say, but she was so bowled over by his sudden change in personality, she wasn't entirely sure what to make of it or how to respond.

It took a few moments for her to gather her wits, at which point Mr. Snypes was long gone.

Muttering her disapproval, she went to work, returning all the books to the vacant spots on the shelves as expediently as possible. What baffled her most was the lie Mr. Snypes had told her, because she very much doubted James had sent him to riffle through all the pages of his books. Which begged the question, why? Why would Mr. Snypes say something she could easily check up on by simply asking James about it? Unless he'd been thrown so far off balance by her arrival, he'd blurted the first thing that came to mind.

"I do hope you are putting all those back in their original position."

It was Jane's turn to be startled by a masculine murmur. Shifting, she looked to the doorway to find Lord Rockwell leaning casually against the frame. "Of course," she told him crisply, hoping her cool response would dissuade him from joining her.

It did not.

Straightening, he sauntered forward like a jungle cat on the prowl. "It really is a shame," he said while she continued tidying up.

She knew she shouldn't take the bait, so she refrained.

But that did not stop him from continuing. "You are far too pretty to be a simple maid, Jane."

A cold shiver scurried over her shoulders. She did her best to appear unaffected. "There is nothing simple about being a maid, my lord. It is hard work and even requires some skill if one is to excel at it."

"Is that what you are hoping to do by keeping Camden's company? *Excel* at it?"

She knew what he was implying and felt her cheeks flush, which only rankled her nerves even further. "There is nothing wrong with exchanging the occasional word with one's employer."

He gave a snort. "I begin to wonder if that is all you are doing." Before she could respond, he said, "Far be it for me to judge since I have enjoyed my own fair share of housemaids over the years. You, however, are exceptionally delightful. I shall have to ask Camden if I can enjoy you when he's had his fill."

Outraged, Jane turned to him with a glare while clutching the book she held firmly to her chest. "You are a disgusting creature, Rockwell."

"Oh dear." He chuckled. "It would appear as though I have struck a sensitive chord with you, Jane."

"Any woman would be insulted by your implication."

"What? That you might be willing to hop from bed to bed? It is a fair assumption considering the speed with which you have taken up with Camden."

"I have *not* taken up with him!"

A sly grin was Rockwell's immediate response, unsettling Jane even further. He turned for the door and thankfully started to leave, but right before he did, he stopped to say, "Then what on earth was he doing in your bedchamber last night?" And with that startling question and a bit of dry laughter, he departed, leaving Jane with an overwhelming degree of shame.

He knew, and given the sort of man he was, it was only a matter of time before others would as well, which meant Jane's days as a respectable woman were numbered. Oh, if only a portal would open up soon so she could escape this place where the slightest lapse in conduct could lead to extreme prejudice.

Spending time with Harrington was no longer

as natural as it had once been. Not after the insight Jane had given James to Harrington's sexuality and the feelings he supposedly harbored for him. In fact, it felt bloody awkward. Yet James did his best to converse with his friend over breakfast. It was just the two of them at the table since Rockwell had already finished his meal before they arrived.

"I take it Lady Elise will be arriving later today," Harrington said as he stuck his fork into a piece of egg and popped it into his mouth. "She would make an excellent match for you, I should think."

James winced while chewing on a piece of bacon. He washed it down with a sip of coffee. "My mother seems to think so, but I disagree. It was wrong of her to go behind my back and ask Rockwell to issue the invitation."

"I suppose she wants what is best for you."

"No. She wants what is best for her and for the earldom. As for me, I am simply supposed to sacrifice my happiness as she did and suffer a marriage of convenience for the rest of my days when—" He broke off, unwilling to divulge too much.

But Harrington stared at him from the opposite side of the table. "When what?"

"It is nothing." Lowering his gaze, James busied himself with buttering his toast.

"Oh my…there is someone else!"

James raised his gaze to meet his friend's. He clamped his teeth together until the tension began to ache and then sighed. "Not exactly, but there is certainly someone with whom I feel the sort of connection a man might want to feel with his partner for life. The problem is, the woman in question is not entirely convinced she would want to be my wife. And that is without considering the ramifications of marrying her." He held Harrington's gaze. "She is not of my social class."

"Is it the maid? Jane?" When James reluctantly nodded, Harrington said, "I have seen the way you look at her. But I have also seen the way she looks at you. Whatever her reluctance may be, it has nothing to do with not wanting you, Camden, because I can assure you she wants you very much indeed."

He knew this of course, but to say as much would take the conversation down a path he would rather avoid, so he simply nodded and asked, "What would you advise?"

Harrington kept silent for a while, the only sound in the room that of their respective cutlery clattering upon the plates as they each continued eating. Eventually, his friend said, "Few of us get what we want in this life. There are many who suffer without ever knowing what it might be like to marry for love. So if you have the strength to make it work, to face the storm that is sure to follow, then I would advise you to court Jane or…Miss Edwards, as you prefer to call her, as if your future happiness depends on it. Because it does."

"So you would support me in this? You would make no attempt to dissuade me?"

"Why should I? You are after all a wealthy man, so it matters not if she is poor. The most important thing, I should think, is whether or not you can accept getting shunned by your social circle. Because I doubt the majority will welcome Miss Edwards. Rather, they will snicker and gossip behind her back and call her a fortune huntress, possibly worse."

James's chest began to ache. "I am aware. But I was thinking perhaps she and I could make new friends, keep to the country, and avoid the gatherings where she might be ridiculed."

"It is possible, to be sure, and of course you will not lose *all* of your current friends either. I shall happily welcome both of you at Long Moor whenever you feel inclined to visit the Lake District."

Appreciating his support, James thanked Harrington, took another sip of his coffee, and turned the conversation toward a fire he'd read about in that morning's paper and how it affected the poor people of London, many of whom were now without roofs over their heads. It relaxed James, knowing that in spite of what he now knew about Harrington, the two of them could still be friends without having to touch on a subject which would likely embarrass them both and perhaps even cause Harrington to break his connection with James.

By the time they stood up from the table, James felt as though all was right with the world. He would talk to Jane, make a proper proposal, and insist that after what happened between them last night, she would have to accept him as her husband and damn whoever failed to agree.

After searching for her, however, and failing to find her, he decided the best course of action might simply be to go to his study and ring the bell. But unfortunately, it was Margaret who arrived. "My lord?" She waited for him to issue instructions.

"Do you know where Miss Edwards might be?" Realizing there was nothing Jane would be able to do on a professional level that Margaret could not, he added, "There is a matter I need to discuss with her."

"I believe she is cleaning out one of the supply closets at the moment. I'll send her up right away."

She moved to leave but James quickly stopped her. "You told me earlier that you were upstairs in my sister's bedroom, the evening she died."

"Yes, my lord." Her expression dimmed. "I was putting away some mending of hers at the time. As I told Jane, I heard the scream, but it wasn't her ladyship. It was someone else."

James nodded. He and Jane had discussed this possibility before. "Did you look out of the window by any chance?"

"I did, but I saw nothing. That side of the terrace was hidden from view. By the time I got downstairs, I saw you and Mr. Snypes hurrying through the hallway with Hendricks on your heels. The rest…" She seemed to struggle now with the words. "I was devastated when I discovered what had happened. Her ladyship was such a lovely woman."

It was what the entire staff had told him, yet someone must have disagreed enough for murder to be a viable option, whatever the motive. "Can you think of anyone – any *man* – who might have had cause to harm her?"

Margaret shook her head. "No. It seems absurd to suppose anyone here might be capable of such a thing."

"Yet someone was, so if there is anything you can tell me, even the tiniest detail, I would be immeasurably grateful."

"I am sorry, my lord, but I—" She bit her lip and James froze, aware she'd thought of something she hadn't yet told him. "I'm sure it's nothing, but there was a rumor going around that Mr. Snypes was madly in love with her."

James felt his stomach roll over. "Snypes?"

Margaret's eyes went wide. "You must forgive me, my lord, it's not in my nature to spread gossip, especially not when I don't know if it's true. Please don't tell him I said anything. I—"

"So my sister never mentioned it to you? She never gave you any reason to believe that she and Snypes were romantically involved?"

"Heavens no! She was a lady and set on marrying Harrington."

Except she hadn't loved Harrington. She'd loved Mr. Thompson. Who was to say her affection for him had not shifted to Snypes after Thompson's departure? Expelling a sigh, James dismissed Margaret and leaned back in his chair. It was becoming clear to him that he had not known his sister very well, a thought that made him feel increasingly depressed, for he'd always thought of her as his confidant. The sentiment obviously hadn't been mutual.

A knock on the door a few minutes later heralded Jane's arrival. She entered slowly and hesitated when he asked her to close the door.

"What we need to discuss must remain private," he explained. "We cannot afford being overheard."

She nodded dimly and did as he bade, then accepted the proffered seat. "It is just that I fear what people might think." When he raised an eyebrow, she said, "Rockwell knows you were in my bedchamber last night. He confronted me about it."

James's every muscle grew taut. "Did he threaten to expose you?"

"It is worse than that," Jane said. "He suggested I hop into bed with him after you're done with me."

"Christ!" Clenching his fists, James rose to his feet and crossed to the window. The urge to punch something, preferably Rockwell, was fierce. It prompted his muscles to bunch and his posture to stiffen while blood pumped rapidly through his veins. "I will have a word with him." He'd call him out, if necessary. Pistols at dawn.

That instinctive thought set him back on his heels. He was by nature a rational man. He'd never allowed emotion to cloud his judgment. And yet, where Jane was concerned, the thought of her with another man, the very idea that Rockwell had so boldly propositioned her, made him want to spit nails.

Disturbed by his lack of control, he inhaled deeply, determined to regain some measure of composure. He turned to face her. "How would he even know you and I…" Words failed him when he noted just how distressed she looked. Hell, the whole situation embarrassed him as well. Because it was not something he'd wanted to share with anyone. It was a private matter between himself and Jane.

"He says he saw you enter my room," she explained.

James frowned. Feeling a need for fortification in the wake of such an unexpected piece of information, he reached for a nearby decanter and filled a glass. "Brandy?" She shook her head so he sipped the spicy drink himself. "The question then, is what he was doing in the servant's quarters last night."

Jane gave him a frank look – the sort that suggested she was about to be brutally honest with him. "He was probably looking to do the same as you."

Every cell in James's body revolted against such a blunt description of what had passed between them in the privacy of her small bedroom. "No. I dare say he was not looking for the same thing at all, Jane."

Her cheeks flamed. "I was not trying to compare your motives to his."

She bit her lip, drawing his gaze to that part of her face and making him long to feel her kisses again. "I should hope not," he muttered, "because Rockwell has never bothered to pretend he does not pursue bed sport at every given opportunity or that he has no interest in love or marriage, while I…I would appreciate an emotional attachment, Jane. Indeed, I felt one with you last night and…" He set his glass aside and crossed the floor to where she was sitting.

Reaching for her hand, he held it lightly between his own, loving the feel of her delicate fingers. "These calluses are new," he muttered, smoothing his thumb over every tip.

"An unavoidable hazard of having to work with your hands," Jane said.

She smiled up at him, but in this instance, the humor in her eyes did not compel him to share that smile. Instead, he lowered himself to one knee and brought her knuckles to his lips. While holding her gaze, he kissed each one in turn, thrilled by the way her lips parted in response. Briefly, he closed his eyes and sought strength from within before looking back up and stating his intentions.

"You are everything I have been looking for all of my life, Jane. Your honesty, your support, your kindness and loyalty compel me to ask if you will do me the greatest honor in becoming my wife." When she opened her mouth to speak, he cut her off by adding, "I know you are not from here. I know you wish to go home. But what if you never get the chance to do so? Would you live out your life here alone then, denying us both the happiness I know we can have together"

She kept quiet a moment and when she spoke, it wasn't to give him an answer, but rather to offer some information. "Your mother has warned me to stay away from you, James. She says she can make me leave if I do not do so."

Of course he should have considered how his mother might respond after he'd told her of his intentions to seek a future with Jane by his side. He winced at his own foolhardy negligence in preventing her from confronting Jane. "She would suffer my wrath for all of eternity if she were to try such a thing. Her only hope was to scare you, but it would seem she underestimated you, for you are not so easily scared. Are you Jane?"

"I am afraid of having to remain here forever. I cannot deny it."

"Even if staying here means you and I can be together?"

When she nodded, it felt like a blow to his gut. He should not have been surprised or upset by her response, but damn it all the same, he was. Tightening his hold on her hand, he decided that perhaps, if he was to have her, he would have to be the one who sacrificed everything. "What if I come with you then?"

Her expression turned from mournful to incredulous. "You would do that for me?"

In that instant, he knew he would sell his very soul to the devil if he had to. It defied all explanation, all common sense and logical reasoning. Which could only mean one thing. He was in love.

The knowledge struck him completely unawares, pushing him entirely off balance. "Yes." Not just in love, he acknowledge while gazing up into her hazel eyes where greens and browns came together in a mesmerizing combination, but utterly, madly and beyond saving, in love.

Wonder filled her gaze. "You are the most amazing man I have ever known," she told him plainly. "But what of your earldom? You cannot mean to sacrifice its future for me, a woman you've known for such a short period of time."

"There is a distant cousin who can inherit. I grant you it is not ideal, but it would be a viable solution. And perhaps this travelling through time thing can happen more than once? Who is to say we cannot travel back and forth on occasion once we figure out precisely how it is done?"

"I don't know," she confessed. "I never thought of that as a possibility."

"Well, it might not be, but then again, it could be. For me, however, the most important thing is for us to stay together." Reaching up, he cupped her cheek with his hand and gently brushed her smooth skin with his thumb. "Losing you forever is too unbearable a thought. So if you cannot stay, let me come with you."

She stared back at him for a long moment, pain brightening her eyes until they glistened. "I cannot do so, James." His heart sank. "Not when you have no idea what you are getting yourself into – what you will face."

He tried to smile even as he felt her slipping away. "Did Columbus know what he was getting himself into when he chose to sail across the Atlantic? Did he know what he would face? Or what of these men you have told me about, the ones who have been to the moon?" Brushing aside a tear as it spilled onto her cheek, he told her simply, "Life is filled with uncertainty, Jane, but there is one thing I do know for sure. You are the woman I want to share my future with, even if that means sailing across the ocean of time."

CHAPTER TEN

IT WAS A BEAUTIFUL SPEECH, the most heart-felt declaration of affection she'd ever heard, even if *I love you* had not been spoken. But it had been implied and the words, infused with need and desperation, had been directed at her, as if she'd stepped onto the pages of a Regency romance novel to be charmed by her very own gentleman suitor.

And she had been charmed. So much so she'd shed a few tears in the process. This was what it ought to be like when a man declared his feelings for you. When Geoffrey had proposed, he'd casually said it while washing the dishes one evening after dinner and in the same tone as when he spoke of current events or a movie he'd like to see. There had been no wish, no yearning or magic. It had just been the next logical step in their relationship, and she'd gone along with it because that was what women did at her age when they'd been dating a guy for a couple of years.

With James it was entirely different. For one thing, he'd needed less than a week to determine she was the one. And while she suspected he might be the one for her too, she wasn't sure if she felt as strongly for him as he did for her. In fact, she knew she didn't. How could she, when she was unwilling to make the same sacrifice as he? And she at least knew what she would face if she stayed here, while he would travel into the unknown if he came with her.

"How can you be so sure I'm worth it?" she asked.

The corners of his eyes creased a little as he smiled, and then he placed one hand over his heart. "Because I feel it here."

She nodded, pretending she understood, even though she feared she didn't. Everything about this whole situation terrified her. Then again, as he'd said, whether or not she would ever be able to leave this time remained to be seen. If she had to stay, what better life could she hope for than one with him by her side? And if she wanted to have a relationship with him without being his mistress, or just a maid he occasionally slept with, then marriage was the only possible option.

So she drew a deep breath and quietly nodded, her mind made up. "In that case yes, James. My answer is yes. I will marry you if you are willing to endure the scandal."

His response was immediate. Without hesitation he pulled her out of the chair and down to the floor so he could kiss her as thoroughly as Rhett Butler had kissed his Scarlett in *Gone with the Wind*. They hadn't lived happily ever after, but Jane refused to think about that as she wrapped her arms around James's neck and returned his kiss with equal fervor.

Perhaps this could work. Perhaps they could build a life together and have the happily ever after she'd always dreamed of. And yet uncertainty remained, lodged at the back of her mind and preventing her from surrendering herself completely.

"Regarding your friend," she said a while later, deliberately burying the guilt she felt beneath the continued need to find the man responsible for Tatiana's and Betsy's murders. "I suspect I know who he was visiting last night."

James helped her to her feet. "Margaret?"

"I believe so. Yes."

James nodded. "I should have known inviting him here would lead to this. The man cannot go two days without tupping a woman."

A thought occurred to Jane, one she knew she had to voice even though it would likely cause offense. "You don't suppose he tried to…you know…with your sister, do you?"

"God no! Rockwell may be a scoundrel, but his friends' female relations have always been off limits. Not to mention he would never consider an inno-cent lady because of the repercussions there would be if he got caught."

"I was thinking that if he did try something and she refused him, threatened to tell you about it even, it might have enraged him enough for him to accidentally—"

"Stop." He gave a disapproving frown. "One does not accidentally slit another person's throat, Jane."

"No," she conceded. "I don't suppose one does."

"Look, I realize your experience with Rockwell has not been then best, and I can assure you he will apologize to you for that before the day is done, but to think he had anything to do with Tatiana's death is madness." He pushed his fingers through his hair. "I have known Rockwell all my life, longer than Harrington. Our parents were friends, their town houses in London a stone's throw from each other, so our nannies would often arrange for us to play."

"Then we'll have to consider other options." In a way she was thankful to have ruled out Harrington and Rockwell, because she knew how difficult it would be for James to deal with if it had been one of them. Discovering it was a trusted servant would be no simple thing either, but it would be easier, she suspected. "Mr. Snypes demands a second glance, if you ask me."

James knit his brow. "Snypes has been in my employ for years. I would trust that man with my life, Jane."

"Would you?" She knew she was about to burst this illusion, but so be it. "Perhaps he told me the truth then, when I found him riffling through books in the library. He said he was looking for something on your behalf."

There was a pause, and then James quietly said, "No. I never asked him to do such a thing."

"Well, he appeared quite frantic about it, manic even, as if his life depended on finding whatever he sought."

"Then I shall have to speak with him as well. Find out the truth." James sank into his chair with a look of exhaustion. A knock at the door swiftly followed, provoking a sigh from James before he called for whoever it was to enter.

Hendricks stepped in. "My lord, Lady Rockwell and her daughter have arrived, as has Mr. Thompson. Shall I show them into the parlor for some refreshment and tell them you will be with them shortly?"

"Yes." James stood as if rejuvenated by this bit of news. "By all means, Hendricks. Thank you."

The butler departed without closing the door behind him. Jane turned to James, unable to hide her surprise. "Tatiana's tutor is here?"

"I sent for him immediately after you made me aware of the note he wrote to her. If the two were as deeply involved as I suspect they may have been, Mr. Thompson might help shed some light on my sister's most private thoughts. Because she obviously failed to share them with me."

Sympathizing, Jane stepped forward, intending to hug him, then recalled the open door and the fact that hugs weren't really a thing in 1818. Especially not between an employer and his employee. So she let her hands fall to her sides again.

"Then you must go and greet your guests," she said. "In the meantime, I shall have a word with Margaret and see if our suspicions about her and Rockwell are true before you confront him."

"Jane…" He paused as if trying to find the right words. With a hasty glance at the doorway, he lowered his voice to a whisper. "Now that you and I are affianced, it seems improper for you to continue with your duties. I ought to speak with Mrs. Fontaine and have you relieved so you can return to a finer bedchamber, dress more appropriately, and allow me the opportunity to romance you as you deserve."

She blushed, quite liking the idea of him romancing her. "Thank you, but until your sister's murder has been solved, it might be best if we keep our engagement a secret." His glower conveyed what he thought of *that* idea. "It allows me to ferret out information from the servants that they wouldn't otherwise confide in me if I was suddenly raised above them."

Pressing his lips together, he seemed to ponder her idea. Eventually, he nodded. "Very well. I will agree with that for now. But if we haven't progressed with our investigation within the next week, I will insist on announcing our engagement so we can begin planning the wedding."

Sensing he would not budge on the issue, she chose to agree. "Okay." He gave her a curious look, and she realized she'd accidentally used a modern word. "It's a substitute for 'very well'," she explained with a wave of her hand. And then, "Since time is of the essence, we will simply have to apply ourselves to the task."

"Agreed." Dropping a hasty kiss on her cheek, James quit the room and went to tend to his duties while Jane went off in search of Margaret.

"How on earth did you guess?" Margaret asked when Jane confronted her ten minutes later. The usually composed maid looked thoroughly flustered as she fidgeted with her skirt.

"It was something he said," Jane told Margaret. She'd deliberately pulled her into the dining room where the two of them made a pretense of polishing a pair of candlesticks while they talked. "He alluded to being in the servants' quarters last night so I made a guess."

Margaret winced. "He promised complete discretion." She rubbed the silver candlestick with increasing vigor. "The man can charm the skirt off any woman he desires. Resistance was utterly futile on my part, Jane."

"I can well imagine," Jane muttered. She'd met her fair share of men like him in New York bars. "Were you with him the night Tatiana died?"

Margaret shook her head. "No. I told you the truth about that night. You have to believe me." When Jane nodded, she quietly added. "Honestly, I should have been stronger, all things considered."

Jane's ears perked up. "How do you mean?"

"Well, it's not as if I'm the only girl around here who caught his fancy, so when he told me I was the prettiest thing he'd ever seen, I should have been smart enough to know it was just a trick to get me into bed."

"I'm sorry." And she meant it. What Rockwell was doing was wrong. "Who else did he compromise?"

"I...I shouldn't really say," Margaret told her, averting her gaze. "It will affect the way people think of the woman if word gets out."

"Please tell me, Margaret," Jane urged. "It might be important." Perhaps it would give Rockwell the alibi he needed.

"It's not really the sort of thing I ought to divulge to anyone, Jane." The conflict going on inside Margaret's head was clear. Eventually she made her decision and said, "I know he was having it on with Betsy from the day he arrived here and until she..." Margaret's words died and her shoulders slumped. "She was smitten by him, always giggling when he was near and doing her best to be the one who cleaned his room and readied his bath.

She made no effort to push him away. Quite the contrary."

"So then perhaps he and Betsy were together that night." Jane voiced the idea out loud without thinking.

"I know she went to his room," Margaret said. "She told me so."

In which case Rockwell couldn't have killed Tatiana. But it did confirm the fact that someone had killed Tatiana in the evening and then killed Betsy later, either that same evening or early the following morning. But who? Jane shook her head. "You know, I'm having a heck of a time figuring out who killed these two women."

"Perhaps you should leave it to the magistrate then," Margaret suggested.

Jane scoffed at the idea. "That man was called upon as soon as Tatiana's body was discovered, and he has yet to arrive. Apparently, he is away on business, though God knows I can't imagine what sort of business would keep him from showing up at an earl's home to help with a murder investigation. Not to mention that whatever evidence there is will have vanished by the time he gets here."

"I know. It's just…your involvement has made the rest of the servants wonder about your relationship with Camden. You seem quite…familiar with him."

"He asked me to help on account of my objectivity," Jane explained. She had no desire to get into details about her feelings for James or his feelings for her or the fact that they had agreed to marry. "My lack of history with everyone here allows me to consider each person with complete detachment."

"Oh." Margaret's expression turned glum.

"That doesn't mean I haven't found friend-ship here," Jane hastened to say. "You have been extremely helpful and kind to me, Margaret. I enjoy your company and hope to continue doing so for a long time yet."

This seemed to enliven Margaret's features. A broad smile fell into place. "I would like that, Jane." She grinned a little. "Just promise me that won't change when you marry his lordship."

Jane froze. "Marry his lordship?"

Margaret's grin turned to laughter. "You ought to see your face right now! Oh, come on, Jane, it's clear to see for anyone who's looking. He's obvi-ously quite in love with you."

"But that would hardly mean marriage," Jane said, reminding Margaret of class differences and responsibility.

But Margaret merely scoffed. "He's an honorable man, as good as they come. If he loves you, he'll marry you. I've no doubt about it."

Well, perhaps Jane ought to enlist Margaret's help more when it came to solving the murder. She obviously had some investigative skills of her own and a keen sense of what was going on, no matter how unlikely that 'what' might be.

"There you are," Hendricks said as he stormed into the room. "His lordship and his guests intend on spending the afternoon out on the lawn with a game of pall–mall. You are to ensure some fresh lemonade is prepared and brought out along with some biscuits and cucumber sandwiches."

"Of course," Margaret told him as she set a

gleaming candlestick back on the table. "We will see to it right away. Won't we Jane?"

Jane nodded and followed Margaret from the room. They returned to the kitchen and prepared two trays with refreshments before heading out to the area where everyone was seated. Following Margaret across the freshly sheared grass, Jane regretted telling James to wait with announcing their engagement as soon as she laid eyes on Lady Elise.

The girl was simply stunning, the very image of a china doll decked out with bouncy curls and layers of lace-trimmed muslin that flowed around her delicate figure like mist around an elven princess. And the way she looked at James, with huge brown eyes filled with endless wonder and lips that smiled just enough to brighten her features without distorting her face, was enough to make Jane lose her cool. Jealousy whipped through her, freezing her lungs so drawing breath became painful.

She'd never felt quite like this, so out of sorts over a man, so ready to fight tooth and nail in order to have him. The emotion was so overwhelming and out of the ordinary, it rather disturbed her to know she was capable of wanting to push another woman aside with physical force in order to lay claim to the man she wanted. It was primitive and it was…she wasn't sure what, but it made her entire body shake, which in turn caused her to spill a bit of the lemonade she was pouring on Lady Rockwell's gown.

"You foolish girl," Lady Camden snapped while Jane hurried to gather some napkins and help blot the stain.

"I'm so sorry," Jane muttered.

Lady Rockwell shoved her hand away. "You, my dear, have done enough. Leave it be."

"Perhaps you ought to return inside," Lady Camden suggested. "We can manage quite well with Margaret's help. Yours is certainly *not* needed."

Catching a slight movement out of the corner of her eye, Jane saw that James was about to interfere, so she rushed to say, "Of course." Meeting his gaze, she gave a hard stare to dissuade him from coming to her rescue, then bobbed a curtsey and walked back up to the house.

James watched a yellow-striped wooden ball roll across the lawn. It missed the wicket it was supposed to pass through, which gave James a small measure of satisfaction. For the ball belonged to his mother, and in his opinion, she deserved a little bad luck after the way she'd treated Jane.

He'd intended to put her in her place as soon as it had happened, but Jane had made it clear she did not want him revealing his feelings for her in front of his guests. So he'd refrained, though doing so did not sit well with him. Rather, it made him feel as if he'd turned his back on her. Part of the reason why he'd refused to join the rest of his party for the game they now played.

Another part was his reluctance to spend additional time with Rockwell at the moment. Confronting his friend about his misguided treatment of Jane had not been easy. It had revealed more than he'd wished to.

"I apologize," Rockwell had said. "I wasn't aware

your arrangement with her was permanent."

"It's not an arrangement," James had clipped.

Rockwell had stared back at him. "Call it what you will, my friend, but you have to know it can never be anything more than a bit of fun."

"Whatever your opinion on the matter, I suggest you keep it to yourself," James had told him.

"Duly noted," Rockwell had said. He'd eyed James with increased uncertainty. "Should we clear the air with a bit of boxing like we used to back in the day?"

Liking that idea, James had welcomed the suggestion and the physical exertion that had followed. It had allowed him to forgive his friend's behavior, especially after landing a satisfying blow to Rockwell's jaw.

A bruise had appeared, more evident now outside in the sun. James tracked the next striped ball with his eyes. "Would you like to take a look at the horses?" he asked Mr. Thompson whose own lack of interest in playing pall-mall had prompted him to remain seated as well.

"Certainly," Mr. Thompson replied. "I could do with a walk."

So could James. Plus, he wanted to speak with Mr. Thompson privately, without the chance of anyone else overhearing, and on a far more important subject than the pleasantries they'd been exchanging thus far.

Neither said much as they crossed the lawn and strode out onto the driveway. The crunch of gravel beneath their feet was a startling contrast to the soft tread they'd made on the grass seconds earlier.

"I must tell you how shocked I was to hear of

your sister's passing," Mr. Thompson said as they walked toward the long stone building from which the sound of whinnying and neighing could be heard. His voice was controlled, as if he strove to force a sense of coolness he did not feel. "I meant to offer my condolences earlier, but with my arrival colliding with that of Rockwell's family, I did not have the chance. For which I hope you will forgive me."

"Of course." They reached the stable building and approached the first stall, where a chestnut colored mare awaited their attention. James picked up a carrot from a nearby bin, broke it into smaller pieces and offered it to her one piece at a time. "For the sake of expediency, allow me to be direct with you." The mare nuzzled his hand, and he moved it, stroking her slowly from muzzle to cheek. "A note was found, addressed to my sister. It spoke of a deep affection on the part of the man who wrote it." When Mr. Thompson failed to respond, James said, "I believe you were in love with her, Mr. Thompson. Perhaps she was in love with you too. What I need is for you to enlighten me. It is clear I did not know Tatiana as well as I thought I did. But the more I discover about her, the more likely I think it will be to catch her killer. So I need you to tell me everything you can about your rela-tionship with her."

A long pause followed. It was so long James finally glanced in Mr. Thompson's direction. What he saw was a face etched in pain. "She was a lovely woman, my lord. Why anyone would choose to harm her…" His voice broke and he looked away.

James returned his attention to the horse, granting Mr. Thompson some small measure of privacy. A shuddering breath followed, and then, "You are correct." The confession was made with astounding honesty. "Tatiana and I fell in love while I worked here, but she was an earl's daughter and then an earl's sister while I...I was – *am* – the simple son of a tradesman. We knew a shared future would be impossible for us, but that did not prevent her from dreaming. And although I urged her to forget me, she continued to write to me after I left, each letter conveying her innermost thoughts, her concerns for the future and how trapped she felt. I could not keep from responding, from offering my support and my undeniable affection."

"In other words, you could not break things off with her."

"I tried. You have to believe me, I tried. But she was like the sun, luring me into the light."

James let his hand fall away from the horse. The analogy was one he could now relate to, for he felt the same about Jane. And wasn't a relationship with her just as impossible as one would have been for his sister and Mr. Thompson?

Needing to move, he started strolling along the length of the stable. When Mr. Thompson fell into step beside him, he quietly asked, "Did you take her innocence?"

Another pause confirmed the truth before the words were spoken. "Yes. And while I know I should apologize for doing so, I cannot, for it was the most wonderful experience of my life."

James shuddered a little, distaste rising in his throat. "She was only sixteen."

"But she knew her own mind. She knew what

she wanted, and she told me so. There was never any doubt, never any risk of me taking advantage."

"Did she tell you about Harrington?" James asked, deliberately changing the subject for fear he might punch Mr. Thompson in the face. But that would cut this conversation short, and James knew there was more for him to discover.

"She wrote she'd found a way for us to be together, though she warned me it would not be ideal." They reached the end of the stable and paused. Mr. Thompson shoved his hands in his pockets. "It would involve her marrying Harrington and keeping me as her lover."

"You never worried over what Harrington might have to say about that?"

Mr. Thompson averted his gaze. A flush rose to his cheeks. "I understand he is a close friend of yours, so I hesitate to say anything that might cause insult."

James snorted and started back toward the other end of the stables. "I want you to speak plainly, man! As plainly as you would speak if there was no risk of being judged. Which there is not. There are other concerns which far outweigh any opinion I might have with regard to what you say."

"Very well then." Mr. Thompson's heel scraped the ground as if in warning. "Some men have no desire for women. Tatiana told me Harrington was one of these men, that he would never want to consummate their marriage and that their union would be for show alone. It was designed to appease his family and would force no restrictions upon her. Indeed, he told her she would be free to take a lover as long as he approved of the man, and that he would claim any children she bore as a result thereof as his own."

"I see." James raked his fingers through his hair. Jane had been absolutely right. Mr. Thompson had just confirmed it.

"There is something else you ought to know, however. Something about your sister I did not approve of."

James steeled himself for the worst. "And that is?"

"She lacked confidence and as such she needed someone to confirm how smart and pretty she was, and…with me gone from here, I suspect she started encouraging the attentions of someone else."

Drawing to a halt, James stared at Mr. Thompson. "Do you know who?" When Mr. Thompson hesitated, James felt the urge to grab him by his shoulders and shake him. Again, he refrained and counted to ten instead. "Well?"

Mr. Thompson nodded. "She mentioned a couple of compliments she received from Mr. Snypes. But the tone of it was not to my liking, for it was clear she held him in low regard. So I started to fear she might be toying with him just to make herself feel better."

This was not the easiest bit of information for James to swallow, for it seemed to suggest that the sister he'd always considered to be the kindest person in the world held a selfish and devious streak. It left him with a sick feeling in his stomach, yet the need to know more remained, like a weight pulling him down into perdition.

"She was obviously flawed," James said, "yet your love for her never wavered."

An unhappy bit of laughter was wrenched from

Mr. Thompson's throat. "Love is a funny thing. It cannot easily be swayed, so no, my love for her never wavered. Rather, it compelled me to sustain our bond, because I realized she needed my guidance. Had I severed all ties as I knew I ought, it would not have helped her at all."

"It would only have pushed her toward a man she did not care for, simply so she could feel cherished." James shook his head, hating the very idea of it, the fragility of his sister's moral compass and the need she'd had for validation. "I should have been here for her or at the very least I should have made sure she spent more time in London than out here in the countryside with only an unfaithful father and a bitter mother for company."

"You are right. It was not the best decision in the world, but you also had your own concerns to consider."

The sentiment was of little comfort. Especially when James considered the time he'd spent here after his father's death. He'd completely ignored Tatiana then, his attention fixed on picking up the reigns and securing a steady income. At the time, he'd told himself he was doing it primarily for his sister, so she could have the dowry she deserved. He now wondered if she wouldn't have been better off with a brother who kept her company, took her out on occasion, and listened to what she'd wanted to say. Especially since Harrington would, all things considered, most likely have married her even if she didn't have a substantial dowry.

"I will have to speak with Snypes now," he muttered, more to himself than to Mr. Thompson.

"If you could refrain from mentioning my name

when you do, I would appreciate that."

Without promising anything, James quickened his step as he strode back to the house. He had every intention of tracking down his man of affairs so he could confront him about his relationship with Tatiana and what exactly it had entailed.

CHAPTER ELEVEN

JAMES FOUND SNYPES IN THE parlor, his hand squeezing Jane's jaw as he pushed her against the wall. "What the hell is going on here?" James's voice carried boldly through the air, causing Snypes to release Jane as if she'd scorched him.

"Nothing, besides the fact that this woman seems to think she has the right to question my actions."

"I confronted him about his reason for rifling through the library books this morning," Jane said, "and I told him I'd mentioned the fact to you, which seemed to enrage him for some peculiar reason."

The sarcasm would have made James laugh if he wasn't so angry at what he'd just seen. He glared at Snypes and then pointed toward a chair. "Sit down."

The man did as he was told so promptly, James might as well have pushed him. "Now, we will get to the whole library incident in a moment, but first, it has just come to my attention that you and Tatiana might have been involved." Jane gasped enough to convey her surprise. "What do you have to say about that, Snypes?"

Snypes glowered to such a degree James imagined fume rising from the top of his head. "We left
notes for each other to find. It was something of a
game we shared."

"So you do not deny that you and Tatiana were
engaged in a relationship that went beyond the
bounds of employer and employee?" James leaned
over his servant. "Did it go beyond the bounds of
friendship as well?"

Snypes tightened his jaw. "Promises were made."

"What sort of promises?" James pressed.

When Snypes refused to answer, James raised his
voice and repeated, "What sort of promises did you
and my sister make to each other?"

"She said she wanted to know if I liked her, all
right?" Snypes barked the words while his face
turned red. "She asked me if I thought she was
pretty." His voice eased a little as he continued. "It
was just one note at first, slipped under my bedchamber door. I passed it back, assuring her that
I thought her the loveliest woman in the world.
Which was true. I did."

"And then what happened?" James forced the
question past his lips while his brain battled over
whether or not to continue this torture. Some
things were perhaps best left alone. But then he
reminded himself that perhaps the man who'd
killed Tatiana was sitting before him right now, and
this gave him resolve.

"It continued like this for a while. Very inno-
cently, though I must confess my feelings for her
began to evolve." Snypes dropped his gaze to the
carpet. "We started placing the notes in different
locations around the house, turning our game

into a treasure hunt of sorts. She seemed to enjoy that. And then…gradually, the messages became more…suggestive."

"Camden." Jane's voice held a note of warning, but James chose to ignore it.

"How so?" he asked.

"She said she wished propriety did not prevent me from holding her hand, then from embracing, then from touching my lips to hers, then…she asked if I ever imagined running my hand up under her skirts, if I thought of her when I lay in bed at night." He released a tortured breath. "I thought she wanted me. I thought she would appreciate my advances, but when I tried to kiss her one time, she drew away, insisting our romance could only exist as it did. On paper."

"So then, when I found you looking through all the books in the library," Jane prompted.

"I was trying to find the last note she'd written because I dreaded the thought of you ever coming across it, Camden, and discovering what your sister was truly like."

This comment earned Snypes a hard punch in the face. James shook his fist and flexed his fingers, feeling his knuckles burn. Straightening, he glared down at the rapidly bruising jaw of the man he'd thought he could trust implicitly. "Did you kill her?"

"No! Of course not." He shook his head, eyes wide and fearful. "I would never do such a thing!"

"You will forgive me if my trust in you has shriveled," James snarled. "You had opportunity and motive."

"No. I was with you when we heard the scream.

Remember?"

"Yes. Except the scream we heard was not Tatiana's. It belonged to a maid who saw her, which means she was already dead and that you could have gone to meet her, argued with her, and killed her before arriving in my study."

Snypes gaped at James. "I swear to you, I did no such thing. Tatiana…God help me I could never harm her." Tears broke past his eyes. "Do you not see that I was in love with her?"

"But she did not love you, did she? And when you realized this, the anger you felt, the momentary lapse in judgment, compelled you to rid the world of her, to destroy the woman who toyed with your heart."

"No," Snypes insisted.

"And when Betsy realized what you had done, you had no choice but to kill her as well. Is that not so?" James shouted the question while Snypes shook his head.

"No. I cared for her. I would never try to hurt her. Please!" He darted a look at Jane as if seeking help from her. "I have always been loyal, but she tempted me, my lord, she…she…" Words failed him as he dissolved into a sobbing mess.

Disgusted, James straightened himself and took a step back. "Ask Hendricks to join us," he said to Jane. "I shall have Snypes confined to his chamber until I am certain he is telling the truth."

Jane did as he bade, leaving James alone with Snypes for a few minutes. "If I find out you are lying and that you wielded the blade that night, there will be nowhere for you to hide on this earth. I shall hunt you down and gut you like the swine you are. Is that understood?"

Snypes nodded and sniveled while frantically searching for the handkerchief which he produced seconds later and put to good use just as Hendricks arrived. James issued instructions, and the butler escorted the suspect out of the room.

"James." Jane's voice broke through the ensuing silence.

He hung his head, his eyes on the tips of his shoes. "I cannot bear to think of her like that," he muttered. "It breaks my heart and angers me at the same time."

She moved toward him, and he suddenly felt her hand upon his arm. "I'm sorry."

He turned slightly toward her, eager to feel the comfort of her warmth. "It seems my sister was a strumpet."

"Perhaps she was simply lost and looking to find her way in all the wrong places."

Sighing, he leaned into her embrace. "I suppose that is one way of looking at it." Raising his head, he met her gaze, his heart unfurling in response to the kind compassion he found there. "Thank you for being my tether, Jane. I cannot imagine what it would have been like to go through this without you by my side."

He kissed her then, long and slow and with all the love he felt for her. "Let me visit you tonight." He kissed the corner of her mouth and she sighed. "I need you, Jane. I need this."

"I need it too," she said, the confession stirring his blood and heightening his anticipation.

Knowing they could not remain like this with the door wide open and a very real chance of discovery, he released her with regret and increased the distance between them. "I will count each second and wish they were passing by faster."

She smiled at that, effectively knocking the air from his lungs. "As will I, *my lord*." Upon which she offered a cheeky grin and departed, hips swaying in the most provocative way he'd ever seen.

God help him survive until tonight.

Jane knew James had obligations. His guests demanded it. And yet, she wished the two of them could simply close themselves away and tell the world to wait. Expelling a weary breath, she wondered what that meant. Was she losing her head over him? Had she already done so? She wasn't the least bit sure. What she did know was that seeing him with Lady Elise made her want to scream or hit something.

Frustration was far too mild a description for how her body and mind were reacting. Her nerves were constantly on edge, her heart ready to explode every time those young, pretty eyes gazed up at James as if he was the most delectable cake Lady Elise had ever seen. It was sickening to watch, even though Jane knew the situation was of her own making.

James had given her a chance, after all, to announce their engagement, but she had refused. Which meant she had no one but herself to blame for her present state of agony. Applying herself to a bit of ironing, simply because it allowed her to escape the company of others for a while, she pondered the riotous storm tearing through her.

She was clearly feeling possessive. The very idea of James so much as kissing Lady Elise's hand was too much to bear. But did that suggest a deeper attachment to him on her part, or was it merely an instinctive need to lay claim to the man she'd bedded – a primitive urge to tell other women he now belonged to her?

She shook her head and proceeded to fold the shirt she'd been working on. She'd never felt so strongly about Geoffrey. Or about any of the other boyfriends she'd had over the years. So why did she feel this way about James? Unless... Blinking, she stared down at the fine linen garment still in her hands. Was it possible she'd never actually loved Geoffrey? That she'd only *thought* herself in love with him because she'd been too distracted by their daily routine? Could it be that what she was feeling now, this rollercoaster of sharp emotion which made her wonder if she was crazy, was what love really felt like?

She'd written about this over the years and had read other authors' descriptions as well of racing hearts and clammy hands, weak knees and shortness of breath, all accompanied by hot embers pricking the skin and butterflies soaring around in the belly. And then, of course, there was that emptiness within when a hero or heroine had to suffer the absence of the person they loved, the way their heart ached and their soul cried out, followed by the completeness they experienced when they were together.

Oh my God!

Jane sucked in a breath and placed the neatly folded shirt on a nearby pile of clothing. She had been feeling all of the above for the past couple of days. And it had been vastly different from anything she'd ever felt for anyone else before. Her feelings for James weren't built on stepping stones of excitement, like moving in together, celebrating birthdays, picking a house, and planning a wedding. Which was how, she realized, it had been with Geoffrey.

With James it was different. She admired him for his kindness and his generosity, for the fact that he cared about people and paid attention to them. She enjoyed simply chatting with him and missed him terribly when he wasn't with her. Like now. And it occurred to her that all she looked forward to with James was sharing each day with him. She didn't need to fill her calendar with things they had to do together or mark her timeline with goals for them to achieve. Just being together was enough.

But what about going home then, a pesky little voice asked.

She wasn't sure she knew the answer to that, for although James had vowed to come with her instead, she knew she would never forgive herself for letting him sacrifice everything for her. She, at least, knew what she would be giving up, but he didn't, and quite frankly, she couldn't quite see him driving a car or using a cell phone or wearing a pair of jeans, a t-shirt, and sneakers. It would be too weird and out of place.

So then what?

Was her love for him – for that was obviously what this was, so why deny it – so strong she'd be able to give up on going home and stay here with him forever? It seemed like an impossible question and an even more impossible decision.

A bell rang and she set the iron aside, hurrying to see where it came from. The parlor, apparently, according to the little plaque placed directly beneath the bell. Making her way through the now familiar hallways and up the servant staircase, she soon arrived in the room to find Mr. Thompson waiting. He was completely alone.

"You called?" She considered the young man who stood by one of the windows. His clothes were not as fine as James's, but that did not distract from his appearance, which was on the high end of the attractiveness scale.

He smiled, the corners of his mouth dimpling in an utterly charming way. It was easy to see why Tatiana would have been drawn to him. Especially if she'd spent two years in his company. She made an inward groan. What on earth had her family been thinking?

"Would you be able to bring me some tea please?"

His question sounded so out of place, as if he half expected her to say no or insist he fetch it himself.

"Of course," she said. "Just give me a moment and I shall be right back."

He thanked her kindly, and she quickly departed, preparing a tray which also contained a small plate of biscuits, just in case he felt like a snack.

When she returned, he beamed at her. "You are a gem." He tilted his head. "Forgive me, but it occurs to me I do not know your name."

"It's Jane, and you are Mr. Thompson," she said, informing him she was well aware of his identity. She reached for the teapot and offered to pour.

"You were Lady Tatiana's tutor, I believe?"

She sensed his silence and glanced his way to find his eyes had dimmed and his smile faded. "I was," he confirmed, "but that is already some time ago now. Five years, in fact, though I fail to believe it."

"Her loss cannot be easy for you," Jane said as she put the teapot aside. "Milk and sugar?"

He gave her a quizzical look, then blinked and crossed to the nearest chair. "Neither," he said as he took a seat. "She was a lovely woman and…" He grew awfully quiet before saying, "What happened to her is unbearably tragic."

Jane hesitated. She ought to leave it at that and depart so he could have his tea in peace. For a maid to remain in a room once her chores were complete was definitely frowned upon. But she knew how much he'd loved Tatiana and reckoned his coming here, to a place filled with memories of her and their time together, couldn't be easy for him.

So rather than take her leave, she said, "I'm a really good listener, if you'd like to talk about it, that is."

His eyes met hers, and he frowned, confirming she'd crossed a line. But just when she thought he was ready to dismiss her, he sighed and nodded. "I think I would like that. If you can spare a few minutes."

As long as Mrs. Fontaine or Hendricks didn't walk in and find her socializing with a guest, she'd be fine. But just in case, she refused Mr. Thompson's suggestion to take a seat and remained standing, ready to pretend she'd been on the verge of leaving if anyone else arrived.

"She loved sunflowers," Mr. Thompson began. Reaching for his teacup, he cradled it between his hands while sipping at the steaming brew. "And Byron." He chuckled lightly. "She was mad for his poetry. And poetry in general, to be fair, but he was her favorite."

"What did you teach her?"

"Mathematics, which she absolutely detested, and a bit of science and literature." He set his cup aside and leaned back in his chair, his eyes taking on a cloudy expression, as if he was staring into nothing. "I fell in love with her, you know. It was not difficult to do so. She was so pleasant to be around, her disposition so positive, and her outlook on life so innocent, it captured my awareness and drew me in a way nothing else ever had. She…" He blinked and focused his eyes on Jane. They were filled with immeasurable sadness. "She was the light in my life, for a while, and the most remarkable part of it all was knowing she felt the same."

"And later, after you left?"

He winced. "We kept in touch, against my better judgment."

"You knew there would be no future for you," Jane said. "She was destined to marry within her own class."

Nodding, he passed the palm of his hand across his face before letting it drop to the armrest. "That is the world we live in, is it not?"

"I suppose it is." She would not press him on this or reveal what she knew regarding the plans they'd had for their future. Instead she said, "It cannot have been easy, sending romantic letters back and forth with none the wiser."

"We had help." He picked up his teacup again and took another sip. "Mr. Goodard became a good friend of mine while I was here. He happily obliged, posting her letters and passing the ones from me on to her. It was not as difficult as you might think."

"Indeed." Jane thought of the footman who kept to himself. He was quiet and private, so she could see why Mr. Thompson and Tatiana would have trusted him.

"When word of Tatiana's death reached me, it crushed my soul. I have not felt the same since and wonder if I ever shall." His eyes took on a suspicious shimmer. "She was the love of my life, the most precious part of it, and with her now gone I…I do not know what I will do."

Jane chose not to comment, because the opinion she'd begun forming of Tatiana was of a woman who toyed with men's emotions, leading them on for her own selfish gain. Which might very well be what had gotten her killed. A sudden thought – a possibility – gave her pause.

She looked at Mr. Thompson. "I am so sorry for your loss. The heartache you feel will never truly go away," she said, speaking of the pain she still felt when she thought of her parents, "but it will get easier over time as you begin to think of it less often."

He nodded. "Thank you for taking the time to hear me out."

"If you ever wish to talk some more, just ring the bell-pull." She bobbed a curtsey and quit the room, intent on finding James, because what if Tatiana had also tempted Mr. Goodard? What if she'd gotten him to help her by flirting with him until she drove him mad with desire?

He didn't seem like the sort to commit cold-blooded murder, but neither did a lot of the people she'd seen on the news over the years, their neighbors declaring they couldn't believe they were capable of such a crime. And yet they were. Perhaps everyone was, given the right set of circumstances.

The point was, they had to consider every possible angle.

But before she could step outside on the terrace and see if James was out there, she was intercepted by Mrs. Fontaine, who asked her to help Cook in the kitchen since Tilly was feeling a bit under the weather.

This kept her busy until after dinner. By the time she was done cleaning the dishes, it was past ten o'clock. So rather than look for James any further, she chose to retire and wait for him in her chamber. But whether or not he came to see her, she did not know. She woke the next morning, aware she'd fallen asleep before managing to read a full page of the book she'd borrowed from the library.

Well, at least she'd gotten a good night's rest and was ready to face the day with a bit more spring to her step than usual. Which was necessary since she had to help not only prepare the breakfast but also serve it. Thankfully, Margaret helped with the trays that had to be brought up to Lady Camden and Lady Rockwell, so Jane would not have to face either woman.

Having to do so this early in the day would definitely put a damper on things, that was for sure.

Still, it did not prevent her from having to face the lovely Lady Elise, who was prettily attired in a stunning riding habit and a cute little hat adorned with a large feather plume.

"I do wish Camden was up," Lady Elise was saying when Jane arrived with a tray filled with plates of food. "But since he is not, I hope you and Harrington will join me for a ride, Rockwell. We could even have a race."

"Sounds like a delightful suggestion," Rockwell murmured while Jane began arranging the plates on the sideboard. "Are you up for it Harrington?"

"Absolutely," Harrington said. "It's been days since I have enjoyed a bit of sport. I could do with the activity, you know?"

With her chore completed, Jane returned to the kitchen. "The guests are having their breakfast and intend to go for a ride immediately after, so I intend to go and clean their rooms now," she told Mrs. Fontaine, who glanced at her just long enough to okay this decision with a nod before returning to the conversation she was having with Cook about that evening's meal.

Leaving them to it, Jane headed upstairs and went straight toward James's bedroom. She had to speak with him about Goodard. So she knocked gently on his door and then slipped inside the room without waiting for a response. And then she froze, because there he was, God help her, sprawled out on the bed face down, so she was presented with the finest view of his butt.

He opened a sleepy eye and squinted in her direction while she quietly closed the door behind her, locking it for good measure because…Jesus!

Anyone could have walked right in and seen him like this. The thought of Lady Elise doing so… Jane's grip on the door handle tightened, even though she knew the other woman would likely have fainted. She certainly wouldn't have known what to do with a naked earl who looked like a mythical God.

Heart fluttering, Jane approached the bed.

A smile tugged at James's lips, and his arm reached out, luring her to him.

"What a lovely sight to wake up to," he murmured when she was within his reach. His hand avoided hers, going instead to her thigh.

"Not as lovely a sight as mine. I assure you." Her voice had gone slightly breathless, no doubt because his fingers were gently massaging her flesh through her skirts. Heat surged inside her, pooling low in her belly and filling her with a shameless amount of need.

He grinned and caught her waist, dragging her down as he turned himself over, so she fell with her breasts pressing into his chest and her legs tangling with his.

"You like seeing me like this, do you?" Wickedness gleamed in his eyes, then he kissed her, ferociously as if he was starved. The effect immediately heightened her own desire, and she greedily kissed him back, loving the feel of his hands in her hair, the warmth and the hardness of his body lying beneath her.

"You're amazing," she whispered, because saying she loved him…well, she wasn't quite ready for that just yet. Not until she was 200 percent sure.

"And you, my little maid, are the most sinful

fantasy come to life." He kissed her again, harder than before while his hands moved lower, tugging at her skirts and reaching beneath until he found the access he sought.

She sighed in response to his touch and welcomed their joining with a groan of pleasure.

"Yes," he murmured while she moved over him, loving him with her body and showing him, without the use of words, how deeply she cared.

It was beautiful in a life-altering sort of way. Much more so than the first time they'd done it, because this time her heart was completely invested. "I cannot stay," she told him regrettably, preventing him from pulling her down to lie next to him when they were finished.

She smoothed her skirts and straightened. Noting the look of adoration in his eyes, her heart thrummed with joy. "Perhaps I should come to check on you more often," she said with a wry grin.

His eyes darkened. "Come as often as you like," he murmured, his tone so suggestive she knew he intended the pun. Which of course made her blush.

She looked away. "Perhaps you ought to get dressed."

He chuckled and she heard the bed creaking and then the tread of footsteps as he moved across the carpet. In another second, his arms came around her in a tight embrace. "What?" he whispered against her jaw, the scrape of his stubble sending a shiver down her spine. "Am I too distracting for you?"

"Yes," she said, not denying the effect he had on her, because really, what would be the point? "And since I have other things to do besides roll around in bed, that's something I can't afford right now."

Making a deliberate effort, she stepped away from him and moved toward the window with the intention of broaching the subject of Mr. Goodard. She heard him sigh, then the rustle of fabric and the sound of him putting on clothes. Drawing the thick velvet curtain aside, she peered out into the grey exterior, her breath hitching slightly in response to the streaks of water trickling down the beveled panes of glass. "It's raining and it looks like the wind's picking up."

Whatever sounds James had been making ceased. Jane placed her fingertips lightly upon the cool surface before her, tracking the path of a plump droplet.

"You should go," he murmured, prompting her to turn toward him. His eyes, so alive with passionate sparks only moments earlier, were dead now, like flames snuffed out in a heartbeat. "It is what you have been waiting for, Jane. The storm to take you home."

"You said." Her eyes began to burn while her throat closed tightly around her words, squeezing until it ached. "You said you would come with me."

He nodded. "I know. But not until I have seen justice served. I cannot allow Tatiana's killer to go unpunished."

She understood. Of course she did. To think it hadn't occurred to her it would be like this, that solving the crime first would be a stipulation, was ridiculous. Struggling for breath while her heart threatened to shatter into a thousand pieces, she returned her gaze to the window. "It's not a storm."

"What?"

"Just some rain and a bit of wind. No thunder or lightening." She allowed the curtain to fall back into place before turning to face him again. But it was awkward now. The compatible ease she'd felt in his company had vanished, overshadowed by her reaction toward the weather. She stepped toward him, hoping to find the right words to appease him, but he was no longer looking at her, his attention on tucking his shirt into his breeches. "James…"

"You do not have to explain it, Jane. I understand how you feel."

"Do you?" Tears welled in her eyes as the distance between them seemed to increase. "Do you know what it is to feel as though you belong in two places at once? What it's like to face a choice, a life-altering decision, that once made might never be undone? To not know which direction to turn because uncertainty lies in both directions, each with the promise of heartache and pain?"

His expression eased, the hard edges smoothed away as compassion entered his eyes. The edge of his mouth lifted, and the look he gave her, so full of pity and something far worse – something final and decisive – ripped her soul from her body. "If you are uncertain about what to do Jane, about whether to stay or whether to go, then I believe you have already made your choice, whether you know it or not."

"What are you saying?" She didn't want him to answer that question and yet she had asked it.

He reached for his vest and put it on quickly, buttoning the buttons with swift efficiency before going to his wardrobe and selecting a jacket. "When it comes to courtship, most men worry over having to compete with other men." He winced while shoving his arms into the jacket sleeves. "It never occurred to me I would have to compete with the future, and frankly, I do not know how to do so or if I even can."

"Then don't." Jane desperately tried to think of the right thing to say. "Let's continue working together, to give you the closure you need so you can be ready to come with me when the chance to do so arises."

Silence swamped her while he stared at her, his dark eyes searching her face until unease crept under her skin. It warned her, before he even spoke, that she'd said the wrong thing and lost him.

"No other woman has ever made me feel as alive as you, Jane. You have challenged me, broadened my horizon, and opened my eyes to the possibility of true love. Sharing my life with you was all I wanted. It seemed so simple, and yet it is the most complicated thing in the world. *Too* complicated, I fear."

"Because I cannot stay?"

"Because whether to stay or to go is even a question for you." His eyes shimmered and he turned away, taking a seat on the bed in order to put on his hose and shoes.

"But, you said you would come with me. I don't—"

"Thinking you would happily make the same sacrifice for me!" He held one hose between his hands while staring down at the carpet. "I offered to give up everything for you because I wanted you to be happy, to have the life you were accustomed to *and* the man who…" His words trailed off, and he suddenly shook his head and pulled the hose over his foot with brisk movements. "It no longer matters, Jane. Our hearts are obviously not aligned."

Tears fell onto her cheeks, and she quickly wiped them away before he could see. "You're wrong about that."

"Am I?" His gaze drove into hers with deliberate force. "Then why are we even having this conversation?"

"Because…because…" She tried to grasp for words that didn't seem to exist. "I cannot stand the idea of having to give you up!"

With a shake of his head, he put on his other hose and proceeded to put on his shoes. "In other words, you want it all without having to sacrifice anything in return. Which brings us back to you not sharing the same affinity I feel, in which case, I fail to see the point of us even trying to be together."

What was left of Jane's heart dissolved into dust. "I was hoping—"

"No. I cannot do this unless I know you love me so much you would give up everything for me. Because that is the only way in which I would ever be able to give up everything for you. The certainty that at least we have each other and the kind of sustainable love that will overcome any challenges is what assured me of my decision. Except I cannot be sure of anything, least of all you or us, when it feels as though your feeling for me is but an illusion."

"That's not true."

"Then stay here with me. Forget your future and be my countess. Let us face the scandal our marriage would cause together."

He was giving her a chance – an opportunity to prove her devotion to him – but she hesitated too long, the uncertainty causing a rift in her brain and making all logical thought impossible.

Seeing this, his eyes shuttered and he strode for the door. "You may remain in my employ as long as you wish, but whatever we shared on a personal basis is effectively over. You may consider yourself free to do as you please."

Jane stared after him as he left, while numbness clung to her body. It sank beneath her skin, filling her with a damp chill and a deep, unrelenting loneliness. He'd broken things off because she hadn't been willing to choose him.

Perhaps he was right. Perhaps she didn't love him enough. She certainly hadn't been brave enough to say she did. As if in a daze, she went through the motions of making his bed while trying to examine her heart. Which was not an easy thing to do when she no longer felt as though she had one. He'd ripped it from her chest and crushed it with his words – with his need for more than what she was able to give.

And yet, she cared for him more than she'd ever cared for Geoffrey or any of the other men she'd dated. She didn't want to have to leave him and never see him again. But to ask the world of him without being prepared to give him the same was selfish. Perhaps it did prove she wasn't good enough for him, no matter how much she wanted to be.

Forcing herself to face this truth, she straightened his sheets and shook out his pillows until she was satisfied the bed looked perfect. Heartbreak was not a pleasant emotion and certainly not a practical one. It had been awful when Geoffrey had called things off and left her, but this was worse. This… She heaved a big breath and forced some measure of control. No. She would not allow herself to dissolve into one of those blubbering women who couldn't think straight because of the hurt they were feeling. All things considered, that would be silly when she was the one who had made the wrong choice. If anyone ought to be heartbroken over it, it was James, whose feelings had not been reciprocated to the extent he had hoped.

Realizing this, Jane made a decision. She would push her own pain aside and focus on the case. The man she'd planned to marry just half an hour earlier had recently lost his sister. Justice had to be served, and so help her, she would do whatever it took to see that through. It was, after all, the least she could do and would hopefully give her something to think about besides mourning the loss of the man she'd been hoping to spend the rest of her life with.

CHAPTER TWELVE

ENJOYING A GAME OF CARDS with Harrington, Rockwell, and Mr. Thompson, James did his best to forget about Jane. But it was impossible. Their conversation earlier in the day, coming right on the heels of an incredible bout of lovemaking, had broken his spirit. It was as if his life had lost its luster, and everything around him was dulled by shades of grey.

Not even his friends' good cheer could brighten his mood, giving him a horrifying insight into the minds of those who chose to end things when it got too hard to carry on. Not that he would ever resort to such drastic measure, but he felt he understood it better now than he ever had before.

Playing an ace, he took the final trick, effectively winning the game. He looked up and tried to smile. "Thank you, gentlemen. Shall we play another round or would you prefer to go for a ride?"

Rockwell frowned. "A ride would be welcome, especially since we were stopped from going this morning because of the rain. But only if you tell us what is troubling you."

James stood, taking the deck of cards with him

with the intention of putting it back in the box where it belonged. It gave him a chance to stall and to not have to face the inquisitive eyes now on him. "I am merely concerned about solving my sister's murder. With each passing day, it seems to grow more impossible."

"Perhaps it was a stranger after all," Harrington suggested. "Maybe a poacher she encountered or a thief she caught by surprise."

Mr. Thompson, whose expression had gone from relaxed to glum at the change in subject, moved his chair back from the table and stretched out his legs. "I would like to think it was not someone she knew and trusted, even if that would mean the man is still out there."

"Perhaps," James conceded just as the door to the parlor opened and his mother swept into the room. She looked as somber as he felt with her black mourning gown and the sort of expression that threatened to scold.

Harrington, Rockwell, and Thompson all stood in order to greet her. She glanced at each of them in turn before pinning her gaze on James. "This house feels like a mausoleum." The comment was gravely spoken, accentuating her words. "Not exactly the ambiance one wishes to strive for when entertaining guests, Camden."

So she *was* here to offer her censure. "What do you propose I do about it?"

Inviting Lady Elise and her mother had been her suggestion, so if she felt they needed entertainment, she could bloody well figure something out on her own. He was already doing his part to ensure the men he'd asked to join him were not bored out of their minds, even though he was starting to wish they would all just leave. Keeping company was no longer something he felt like doing.

"We could visit the assembly room," she declared.

James almost choked in response, prompting a cough from which it took him a second to recover. "I beg your pardon?" His mother detested the local assembly room and had adamantly protested every effort he'd ever made to visit.

"It will liven things up," she said, "make everyone forget about death for an evening."

He stared at her. "You cannot be serious! Going dancing after a death in the family would be highly inappropriate. We need to wait at least a month before engaging in any social events." How could she suggest such a thing when she'd always been such a stickler for protocol?

She waved a dismissive hand. "You need not look as though you are enjoying yourself, if that is what concerns you. Nor do you have to dance, though partnering with Lady Elise for one set would not be so very terrible." She gave a curt nod. "Our guests deserve a bit more entertainment than what we have been providing. We owe it to them as hosts."

"Perhaps—"

"You will not stay home if that is what you are about to suggest. We shall all attend and make the most of it. Is that understood?"

He glowered at her while wondering what it might feel like to tell her to go to the devil. Instead, he said, "You and I will discuss this later." In a more private setting. He certainly had no intention of forcing anyone into such an exhibition.

"No, James. We will not." And with that final

remark, she exited the room like a storm drifting out over the horizon.

Confounded and furious, James stared after her retreating form. She would apparently do anything to pair him off with Lady Elise. But this time she went too far.

"She cannot be serious," Mr. Thompson said when no one else spoke. "You are expected to mourn for at least three months after losing a sister. To attend a dance little more than a week after suffering her loss is unheard of. People will talk and their words will not be kind, Camden."

"I am aware," James said, "which is why I have no intention of going along with this mad scheme of hers. The three of you can attend the dance if you wish. In fact, I encourage you to do so, since a change of scenery will likely do you all some good."

"I prefer not to," Mr. Thompson muttered.

"Tatiana was my fiancée," Harrington said. "It would not be right."

"Then you should take your mother and sister out, Rockwell," James said. "I am sure they will find it diverting."

Rockwell nodded. "Perhaps, though I know my sister will sorely miss you, Camden." He leaned back more in his seat and studied James. "She hopes to receive your attentions, but since her arrival, you have shown little interest."

"Well," James muttered, ignoring the frantic beat of his heart, "that is about to change. See if she wishes to walk with me later today, would you? The weather has cleared. It seems we shall have a pleasant afternoon."

Rockwell inclined his head and smiled. "Certainly." Picking up the glass of brandy he'd poured for himself before the last game of cards, he took a sip. "Nothing would please me more than for us to be brothers."

"Do you know when Mr. Goodard will return?" Jane asked Hendricks.

That morning, with her nerves and emotions in a tangled mess, she'd forgotten to mention her latest findings to James. Or perhaps she ought to think of him as Camden again? No. That would be impossible for her to do after the intimacy they'd shared. Either way, she would proceed with her investigation and see what else she could discover. Speaking with Mr. Goodard was the next logical step.

"In another half hour or so, I should think." Hendricks peered down at Jane in that butlery way of his until she felt like squirming. "Something I can help you with?"

"No. It's nothing urgent," she assured him. "I was merely hoping to talk with him.

Hendricks eyed her carefully, and she wondered if he believed her. She would probably never know since he offered no hint of his thoughts before turning away and heading toward Mrs. Fontaine's office.

Jane went in the opposite direction, taking the servant stairs up to the servant's floor with the intention of cleaning the hallway there. Anything to keep her mind distracted from the anguish of having lost James forever. Because frankly, she couldn't think of what to say to make things right

again between them. After all that had happened
and the words they'd spoken, even if she told him
she loved him, she doubted he would believe her.
The only way to convince him of the contents of
her heart was to show him. Except she wasn't sure
how. Not without opportunity, which she doubted
she'd have since he'd made it quite clear they
would not be spending more time together than
what was required between a master and a servant.
And with Mrs. Fontaine present, Jane believed he
would simply convey any messages he might have
for her through his housekeeper.

Distraught and feeling more lost and lonely
than she'd ever felt in her life, Jane swept the floor.
Knocking on the bedchambers in turn to ensure
they were empty, she entered each room and
cleaned them all individually.

It wasn't until she reached her own bedchamber that she chose to take a break. Leaning against
the wall she tried to banish the hurt that surfaced
whenever a door at the front of her mind creaked
open and memories of James spilled through it.

Placing one hand against her belly, she pressed
against her shuddering nerves in a hopeless attempt
to calm them. God, what an idiot she was. She
loved James, but when it had come down to act-
ing on that feeling, she'd been a coward, running
from the unknown and clinging to something that
might not be hers again.

"Stupid, stupid, stupid." She might be stuck in
the past forever now without even being able to
share it with him.

Annoyed with herself, she glanced out the window and stilled, her eyes following the two people

who walked across the lawn below. Jane swallowed, the effort drawing her awareness to the painful lump in her throat. Because there James was, keeping company with Lady Elise and laughing in response to some delightful thing she was saying.

Jane's nails dug against the palms of her hands as she balled them tightly at her sides and willed away the tears. It was only a few hours since she'd climbed from his bed, the smell and feel of his body moving in time with hers, his whispered words and the mind-numbing pleasure she'd found in his arms so fresh she could practically reach out and touch the memory of it. And then she'd gone and ruined it with uncertainty and a lack of commitment to him. She'd failed to convey how much he meant to her and how agonizing life would be without him by her side.

Because rather than offer immediate assurance, she'd hesitated, weighing her options while trying to envision the various possibilities. And then, to make matters worse, she'd voiced her doubt, leaving no question in his mind that her feelings for him, her willingness to do whatever it took for *them*, did not match his own resolve.

Below on the lawn, James linked his arm with Lady Elise's as the pair moved out of sight. Jane pressed her hand to her mouth, stifling a sob. Searing pain sliced through her chest, and her hand came up, clutching at the windowsill for support while her body shook with agonizing tremors and wet streaks dampened her cheeks. This was all her fault. She had no one else to blame for the pain she was now enduring.

Time heals all wounds. Wasn't that the saying?

She wiped at her tears with the heel of her hands while gulping down a series breaths. Shaking her head, she stared blankly at the cloudless sky before turning away from the window. No. Nothing would ever make this go away. Not even two hundred years. Because somewhere in time, James would still have walked away from her, and that wasn't something she would ever get over.

Hating the state she was in, she determined to pull herself together. James still needed her help. Solving Tatiana's murder and seeing justice served was important to him. Of course it was. And… She straightened her spine, crossed to her dresser, and pulled a handkerchief out of the top drawer. Feeling sorry for herself would get her nowhere. Yes, it sucked that she'd only just realized she loved James with all her heart the moment she'd lost him. And of course, the fact that she wasn't 'right' for him or that they hadn't been meant to be together even though she'd never felt she belonged with someone as much as she belonged with him, was a difficult truth to face.

But she was a New Yorker, damn it, an independent woman who'd kicked a mugger's ass once when he'd tried to steal her purse on the subway. She squared her shoulders and glanced at the small oval mirror that hung on the wall. She'd lost that person in her breakup with Geoffrey and the crazy turn her life had taken since then. Her confidence had dwindled because she'd been out of her element and she'd panicked.

Considering her face which looked so plain without her usual makeup, she made her decision. It was time to buck up, as her mom used to say, and get on with the day. However bad things seemed to be going, she hadn't been arrested or sentenced to death for Tatiana's murder, for which she was undeniably grateful.

She inhaled deeply and blew out a breath. As much as she disliked having to face James right now, he needed to know about Mr. Goodard.

Hopefully whatever the footman had to say would shed some light on the murder and bring them one step closer to solving it.

"You have such a beautiful property, Camden," Lady Elise said, her voice almost lyrical in rhythm.

James knew it was the sort of speech pattern she'd probably spent a decade trying to perfect, pronouncing each word with effortless skill and with a refined delicacy most young ladies would envy. He, on the other hand, hated it, for it conveyed a degree of pretentiousness he'd grown weary of lately. After meeting Jane and growing accustomed to her blatant candor. There was nothing practiced about the way she spoke. She just did it, in the same way the working class did it. And yet, she still managed to convey a higher degree of education and cultural acumen than most of the people he'd met.

"Thank you," he said, reminding himself he ought to respond and at least pretend he was enjoying Lady Elise's company instead of thinking about someone else. "I much prefer it to my London townhouse, not only because it is bigger but because it is not in London."

She glanced up at him in surprise. "You do not

enjoy going to Town?"

"Not really," he admitted. "I only go because I must. When Parliament is in session. But London is a filthy place, and I would much prefer to stay here."

"But…" She glanced away before saying, "There is very little entertainment in the countryside, whereas London has the theatre, the opera, an endless list of social events, museums, teashops, and restaurants."

He understood her, even though he didn't agree. In his opinion it was all a lot of noise and pressure. But she was young, without a property of her own to spend her time and energy on. Of course being in Town would hold greater appeal to her than a quiet life secluded from Society. Perhaps this was part of the reason why Jane found it hard to stay. She'd told him the New York she knew was larger than anything he could imagine. It pulsed with life and had buildings spearing the clouds. Which stood in stark contrast with what he could offer her here at Summervale.

"Nevertheless," he muttered, burying the ache in his heart and the raw wound burning in his chest, "I prefer the peace and quiet available here."

"So then, what you are saying is you would spend as little time in London as possible? No more than what is absolutely necessary?"

"My life is here, Lady Elise. The estate keeps me busy and fills me with satisfaction." He smiled down at her, aware she did not find his comment compelling. "When I am away, I long to return." And yet, he'd been willing to give it all up for Jane, with the chance of never coming back, because he'd fallen in love with her and had foolishly thought she felt the same way.

"If I may be honest," Lady Elise said with a great degree of thoughtfulness, "I cannot see myself living such a life. I know your mother invited me here so we could become better acquainted. My brother has said the most wonderful things about you over the years, and based on the few interactions we have had since the first time I met you, I must confess I thought you would make a wonderful match."

"But the truth is we would make each other unhappy."

"Yes. I believe we would." Coming to a halt, she gazed up at him with the bluest eyes he'd ever seen, leaving no doubt in his mind she would have no trouble at all securing a husband for herself. It just wouldn't be him. "Our interests are not aligned, and while I know Mama and Rockwell would both laugh at me for saying this, I do hope to marry a man with whom I enjoy spending time – a man with whom I long to share my days."

"You hope for love," he told her simply.

"Is that silly of me?" she asked. "Am I being naïve?"

"Not at all." Reaching up, he cupped her cheek with brotherly affection. "You deserve it, and more than that, I can tell you as someone who knows, it is not impossible to find." Even if it didn't always lead to the happily ever after one hoped for.

She smiled with more warmth than he'd thought her capable of, as if the honesty of their conversation had stripped away the façade and allowed him to see the real Lady Elise. "Thank you for confiding in me. I would have hated to get between you and the woman you love."

Appreciating the sentiment even if it felt as though the future he'd hoped to share with Jane was now forever out of reach, he leaned forward, just enough to place a kiss on Lady Elise's cheek. "Thank you," he whispered close to her ear. "I—"

A sudden gasp cut him off, prompting him to straighten and turn just in time to glimpse the grey wool hem of a skirt disappearing behind the corner of the building. *Jane.* It had to be. He dropped Lady Elise's hand as if burned and took a step back. "Forgive me, but I—"

"Go after her," she urged without bothering to hide the pity she felt on his behalf at the sudden realization of who his heart belonged to. "I will be fine. Now hurry." She jutted her chin in the direction Jane had gone, and James forced his feet into motion, hurrying after Jane as quickly as he could and just in time to see the door to the herb garden swing shut.

Following her through to the tiny courtyard where square box planters held all sorts of fragrant plants, James called to her before she managed to pull the door to the pantry open. "Jane!"

She froze, her fingers on the handle while giving him nothing but her back. "What I want to tell you can easily wait until you're no longer busy," she said, her voice so flat it unnerved him.

"I have time now," he said, taking a step toward her.

She kept her body and face averted, refusing to look in his direction and still ready to pull the door open and bolt. "I'm sorry for interrupting your courtship. That was not my intention."

Moving closer still, he studied her posture, the rigidity of her body suggesting she might be forcing herself to stay calm. But if she didn't love him, then… "Jane." He spoke her name softly while reaching past his own hurt in order to try and see hers. "What you saw was nothing more than a friendly bit of reassurance."

She winced. "Is that what you call it?" Her face snapped around, and her eyes, pooling like lakes on the verge of overflowing, met his, stabbing him with equal parts pain and anger and something else – something so much stronger it stole his breath. "You ended things with me and promptly gave your attention to her. And while I know I shouldn't care, while I know I have no right to do so when I don't even belong here and she is everything you need in a wife – the perfect package, so to speak – I cannot ignore the deep sense of the loss I'm feeling inside. It's as if I died today, and all that remains is an empty shell."

His hand settled upon her arm, and without even thinking about what he was doing, he drew her toward him, holding her close while his other hand soothed over her back. "You broke my heart this morning," he murmured.

"I broke my own as well," she choked against his shoulder. "I…This was the first rain I've seen since coming here, the first hope I'd had of ever returning to my own time, and I got carried away with it. I'm sorry."

"And I should have understood that." He knew this now that he'd had some time to think. "I should have known how difficult it would be, impossible even, for you to choose between the life you have always known and a man you only just met one week ago."

Leaning back ever so slightly, she gazed into his face, and although tears clung to her lashes, her eyes conveyed a soul-deep connection he knew he wasn't imagining. And then she said, "It's no longer impossible. In fact, it's really quite clear that I belong where you are James, no matter when that might be."

His thumb stroked across her jaw as her arms wound around his neck. She was the most incredible woman he'd ever known, the most remarkable part of his life, and the fact he'd met her, the odds of it so unlikely, it rendered him speechless. So rather than say what words could not convey, he drew her face to his and kissed her with all the love and devotion that burned through his veins.

She answered by parting her lips and pulling him closer, matching his fervor as he deepened the kissed and pressed up against her. The scent of her was familiar, infusing his senses with sweetness and mending his heart. "Jane." Her name was swallowed by her answering kiss, the hunger and boldness with which she delivered it cutting him off at the knees.

His hands clasped her hip and her back, holding her to him while the heat flowing through him evolved into urgent need, and he started to wish they were anywhere else – somewhere private – ideally in a room with a bed. The throaty moan with which she responded suggested she felt the same, but this was not the place for that. Not when any number of people could come dashing through the pantry door at any moment.

With this in mind, he loosened his hold and took a step back. "May I suggest we forge ahead, heedless of what might happen in the future? Nothing is ever certain, Jane, not even for an ordinary couple. There are always obstacles to overcome—"

"None as challenging as what we face, I suspect." Her hand found his, clutching it tightly. "But you're right. All this time I've been letting fear rule me. It made me sabotage what we had before even giving us a proper chance. So yes, let's forge ahead and see where things lead."

He kissed her again, his happiness overshadowing any threat of scandal their engagement and ensuing marriage would cause, along with the threat of one day losing her. Because loath as he was to face it, he knew deep in his heart that choosing him over going home would not be as simple for her as either of them wanted it to be. For now, though, he pushed that thought as far back as it would possibly go, burying it deep beneath the pleasure of her kiss.

She laughed against his lips, and he pulled back to see her face, illuminated by a ray of sunshine spilling over the courtyard wall. "You're a terrible distraction," she said, playfully slapping his arm. "You almost made me forget what I came to tell you."

"Only almost?" He deliberately arched an eyebrow and infused his smile with a touch of mischief.

Her expression sobered. "Considering the importance of the matter, I'd say your ability to make me forget all about it deserves a pretty high score."

"The things you say." He shook his head, surprised as always by her unusual turn of phrase. Recalling what she'd just told him, he made an effort to focus. "What did you wish to tell me?"

She pulled out of his embrace and crossed her arms as if to discourage him from further intimacy. "Are you aware it was Mr. Goodard who helped your sister and Mr. Thompson with their exchange of letters?"

James stared at her. "Indeed I was not." He thought back on the conversation he'd had with Tatiana's former tutor himself and shook his head. "Mr. Thompson never mentioned it to me."

"Well, I find it kind of interesting that Mr. Goodard didn't say anything either when you questioned him about his relationship to your sister. What was his alibi for the night she died, if you don't mind my asking?"

"He said Hendricks gave him permission to retire early on account of a headache, so as far as anyone knows, he was upstairs asleep."

"But that's not really an alibi, is it? Unless someone checked to see that was what he was doing."

Sighing, James raked his fingers through his hair. "I suppose so, but what on earth would be his motive for wanting to hurt Tatiana and then kill Betsy?"

"How should I know?" Jane's shoulders slumped in response to a deep exhale. She glanced at the sky before looking back at him. "We know your sister was a bit of a flirt."

"She was more than that," James muttered, disliking the reminder.

"So maybe she led Goodard on as well, and he got angry when all she used him for was passing love notes to another man?"

"I don't know, but we should definitely speak with him right away. Or rather, *I* should speak with him." He was already itching to do so, to uncover the truth Mr. Goodard had kept to himself.

"And after that, I suggest you question everyone again while keeping everything you've discovered so far in mind." She gave him a sympathetic smile. "Because no one has left here since it happened, which means if it wasn't a stranger, then whoever committed the act is still here in this house."

CHAPTER THIRTEEN

JANE CHOSE TO TAKE A seat in the corner of Hendricks's small office with the intention of lessening her presence. James had insisted she remain in the room with him while he questioned Mr. Goodard, but the curious, even disapproving look, she'd received from Hendricks confirmed she didn't belong there. Which was to be expected since her position as a housemaid put her on equal footing with Mr. Goodard. She was not his superior and couldn't even serve as a witness to any wrongdoing he might have committed. So of course Hendricks and anyone else who discovered her involvement in the interrogation would wonder about it *and*, consequently, about James's reasons for insisting she join him.

"She discovered some valuable information," James had explained to Hendricks. "Having her here might lessen Goodard's deniability."

Although Hendricks had nodded, his expression had remained skeptical. But he would never question James's decision and had kept whatever opinion he had on the issue to himself, for which Jane was grateful.

"Mr. Goodard," James began as soon as the foot-man was seated on an extra chair they'd brought in. James and Hendricks, on the other hand, remained standing. "How long have you been in my employ?"

The footman blinked as if surprised by the question. He shifted slightly in his seat. "Five years, my lord."

James nodded. "And have you been happy here during this time? Have you been well treated, that is, and fairly compensated for your work?"

"Of course, my lord. I cannot imagine a bet-ter place for employment than Summervale." Mr. Goodard darted a look in Jane's direction, and she deliberately glanced away, refusing to offer support until she knew more.

Shoving his hands in his trouser pockets, James rocked back on his heels and considered the man before him. He eyed Hendricks for a second before asking the next question. "How well did you know my sister?"

Mr. Goodard's eyes widened. A bit of nervous laughter escaped him before he managed to school his features once more. "As well as any other ser-vant, I'd imagine. I mean, my interaction with her was limited to serving dinner for her at the table and running the occasional errand."

James narrowed his gaze on Mr. Goodard. "And what exactly did these errands entail?"

Mr. Goodard looked to Hendricks, but the butler's expression was set in stone. "Answer the question, lad," he advised in a steady tone that brooked no nonsense.

"I...I...I dunno. I would fetch things for her

once in a while, set up her easel on the lawn when she wished to paint, and help carry her boxes when she went shopping." Mr. Goodard's level of discomfort seemed to increase, his fingers now restlessly drumming his thigh. "Why are you asking me this? What's this about?"

James stared down at Mr. Goodard. "It is about you facilitating a romantic attachment between my sister and her former tutor, Mr. Thompson."

Mr. Goodard froze, his mouth hanging open while his eyes took on a dazed appearance. Then he suddenly swallowed and blinked. "She said she had no one else to turn to, no one else she could trust."

"Bloody hell," Hendricks muttered, following the expletive with an immediate apology. "What were you thinking?"

Mr. Goodard flinched but to his credit, he did not shy away from the truth or dissemble in any way. Instead he said, "What was I to do? Betray her trust?"

James rubbed his palm across his jaw. "While I sympathize with the choice you had to make, you must have considered that *I* am your employer, not her. Your loyalty was first and foremost to me."

"I'm sorry. You're right of course," Mr. Goodard said, "but she was desperate. Her love for Thompson was clear and...well, she was so unhappy about it that I agreed to help."

"And it never once occurred to you how inappropriate it was for you to do so?" James's voice tightened. "She was an earl's sister while *he* was no more than her tutor!"

Jane drew a sharp breath, and James glanced

toward her, the angry lines in his face fading fast until his expression turned more apologetic. She shook her head lightly to tell him it was okay, that *she* was okay and that she didn't blame him for stating the obvious.

But Mr. Goodard saw the exchange and straightened in his seat. "They loved each other, my lord," he said, drawing James's attention back to him. "I don't see how that's any different from the affection you share for Jane."

"That is quite enough," Hendricks barked. "How dare you speak to his lordship like that you impertinent pup?"

James held up a hand. "I will let the comment slide if you tell me the truth, Goodard." He paused for effect. "Were you in love with Lady Tatiana as well?"

"No!"

"Did it grate, knowing she loved someone else and having to help her exchange secret letters with that man?"

"Of course not," Mr. Goodard blurted. "If it had I would just have torn up the letters and thrown them away, told her Thompson hadn't written to her, and waited for the whole thing to fade. But I didn't. That's not what happened."

"Unless of course you were torn between helping the woman you loved and keeping her to yourself. Perhaps—"

"I fancy Tilly, all right?" Mr. Goodard's face had turned a bright shade of red. His lips parted and closed in rapid succession, like a fish out of water, until he finally deflated on a long exhalation. "I've had a thing for her since the day I arrived here, and she helped me arrange a tray to your mother's liking."

Silence filled the room and then James took a step back. His lips flattened while he seemingly pondered the truth of what Mr. Goodard had told him, and then he nodded. "You should tell her. Perhaps she feels the same way."

Mr. Goodard shook his head. "I want to. Especially with everything that's been happening. Seeing how out of sorts she was over Betsy's death has been hard. The two were close friends."

So that was why he'd been sulking about? Because he hadn't known how to comfort the woman he loved when he didn't know how she felt about him? Jane wanted to kick herself for being so blind.

"You will forgive me for questioning you, I hope," James said. "With the killer still walking around in our midst, I have to consider every possibility."

"And you thought I might have done it?" Mr. Goodard's eyes were as wide as saucers now. When James's lips twitched, he shook his head firmly. "I could never do such a thing, my lord."

"I know that now," James told him. He gestured toward the door. "You may return to your duties, Mr. Goodard. Thank you for your time and once again, I do apologize for believing it might have been you."

"What now?" Jane asked as James escorted her back upstairs where she was expected to set the table for dinner. "I don't suppose the butler did it?"

The look James gave her made it clear he did not find her comment amusing. "I have no idea what our next step should be, to be honest. It does appear as though Snypes is the one who did it, though instinct tells me otherwise."

"I'm sorry, but I think you might be right." She spoke the words as the two of them exited the stairwell and entered the hallway. "He had opportunity and motive and—"

"Camden!" James's mother bore down on them with a glower while Lady Rockwell followed behind.

James turned. "Mother! What a pleasant surprise."

Jane stifled a grin in response to the sarcastic tone, concealing all traces of humor with a hasty curtsey.

"Considering your reluctance to attend a dance at the assembly room while still in mourning, and forced to admit may have a point, I thought it might be nice if we simply made an evening of it here with those already present." Her face showed no hint of emotion while she waited for him to respond.

"You mean to have a party with only seven people?" James's disinterest was obvious.

"We can easily dance a few different sets. There are certainly enough men and women present as long as the younger gentlemen are willing to partner with us dowagers." She paused for a second as if expecting him to say something to that, but when he didn't, she said, "It will give us something to do besides the usual, and dressing up is always good fun."

"I disagree, but I will happily bow to your wishes if a festive evening is what you desire." He smiled broadly, in that polite way Jane had come to recognize as being completely fake. "Anything to please you and our guests."

"Well in that case," Lady Camden said, her face tightening into a mask of superiority, "perhaps you can tell Jane to go and do what we are paying her to do?"

Knowing what it would take for James to give his mother a set down in front of Lady Rockwell, Jane took a deliberate step back.

"Last time I checked," James stated, "I am the one paying the salaries, not you." He glared at his mother, apparently willing to face both women's censure. Or perhaps he just didn't care what they thought. "Even your stipend is at my discretion and subject to my mood. If I may offer a piece of advice...try to refrain from antagonizing me."

He turned to Jane who silently cheered his response, her heart swelling with pride and love because he'd taken her side over his mother's, which couldn't have been an easy thing to do since it went against proper upbringing and decorum.

Affection emanated from his gaze and the barest of smiles, directed only at her, touched his lips. "I am sure you have somewhere else to be besides here." He gave her a reassuring nod. "I will speak with you later."

Aware her remaining there wouldn't be proper, Jane accepted his suggestive dismissal with a smile, bobbing a curtsey and turning away. And as she entered the dining room, she could hear the continued exchange ensuing between mother and son, the sharp voices suggesting their disagreement was far from over.

Breathing a sigh of relief and silently thanking James for giving her a chance to escape, she closed the door and went to collect a new tablecloth and napkins from a wide marble-topped cabinet while wondering how she would ever be able to deal with having a mother-in-law like Lady Camden.

Resting his feet, James leaned back against his chosen armchair and watched the quadrille currently under way. The ballroom felt huge with so few people present, but the lively tune being played by a musician Hendricks had brought up from the village helped fill the space with a positive atmosphere.

Perhaps his mother was right, loath as he was to admit it. Perhaps a party was the very thing to lift the veil of depression hanging over Summervale. His guests certainly deserved it, and their joyous faces warmed his heart, even as his sister's absence crushed it. She'd always loved to dance, her smile wide and her steps so graceful she'd been the envy of many young ladies and the subject of much admiration.

"You look a bit put out," Harrington said, dropping into an adjacent chair and handing James a glass of champagne. Overhead, the chandeliers sparkled in response to their two hundred candles, which was something of an extravagance for such a small event, even if he did find it worth it.

"I was just reflecting," he said, thanking Harrington for the drink and setting the glass to his lips. He took a sip. "Has it really been a week since she died?"

The viscount puffed out a breath. "I suppose so."

"It seems like forever and yet so recent. I am still not used to the idea of her being gone and wonder if I ever will be." He glanced toward the entrance to the ballroom. "I still expect to see her rounding a corner with laughter in her eyes and a few stray curls bouncing against her forehead."

"And so you shall for quite some time." Harrington's voice turned pensive. "Time makes it easier. It allows us to move on and lessens the severity of the pain. But it never goes away completely. How can it when the person you have lost was an intrinsic part of your life?"

James glanced his way and their eyes met. "How insensitive of me. I forgot about your brother." He'd never met the man because he'd been older than them by roughly ten years and never present the few times James had gone to visit Harrington during his childhood. His death at Waterloo had changed Harrington's life forever.

"As I said, it gets better. We learn to go on without them and perhaps appreciate the time we have and the people we've known more than those who have never loved and lost."

Nodding, James prepared to say something else to lighten the mood, but then the dance ended and his mother approached, forcing him and Harrington to their feet. "The first waltz is about to begin, and Lady Elise is without a partner." She stared at James without blinking.

"Well—"

"Thank you for bringing it to our attention. I have been hoping to partner with her myself," Harrington said. "If you will excuse me." He sketched a quick bow and went to invite Lady Elise to dance while James watched with some surprise.

"Now look," his mother hissed. "Your dillydally-

ing has placed her squarely in the arms of another."
She shook her head. "Honestly, Camden. Do try to
make an effort."

Holding his tongue, James let her go without
a retort. He was still a touch surprised by Harrington rescuing him from his mother's pointless
attempt at matchmaking to bother. The viscount
swept Lady Elise into his arms as the music started
and twirled her about. His gaze met James's and
the edge of his mouth lifted as he winked, conveying without words the calculated purpose of
his actions and perhaps the satisfaction he took in
besting the Countess of Camden.

Having finished helping out in the kitchen, Jane
readied a tray for Mr. Snypes and took it up to his
room. The footman standing watch outside produced a key and unlocked the door. "Your supper
is here," he said without crossing the threshold.

A moment passed and then Mr. Snypes appeared
in the doorway. He glanced at Jane and then at the
tray before taking it from her grasp and preparing
to turn away.

Jane stopped him by saying, "It looks like you did
it, Mr. Snypes." She ignored the footman's presence
and the obvious discomfort Mr. Snypes appeared
to be feeling in response to her blunt remark.
"Proving otherwise doesn't seem possible, so if
there's anything you can tell me – anything at all
that might suggest your innocence and another's
guilt, then I recommend you do so now."

"Why should I when the reason I'm locked in
this room is because Camden didn't believe me

even when I insisted I didn't do it."

Jane fought the urge to roll her eyes. "Your relationship with Lady Tatiana didn't exactly give him much reason to trust you, did it?"

"There's a big difference between exchanging notes with someone and suddenly choosing not only to kill them but to go through with doing so." His voice was low, and yet it conveyed his frustration and perhaps even some measure of regret.

"I know that and so does Camden, which is why he's reluctant to see you hang. But unless you can prove you weren't involved, then that is probably what will happen." She fought her way past the lurch in her stomach and willed herself to say what mattered. "The magistrate will arrive any day now and when he does, he'll be looking over things more objectively than anyone else. He won't fight for you, Mr. Snypes, he'll condemn you because of what you *did* do and how guilty it makes you look."

Mr. Snypes dropped his gaze and stared down at the tray while Jane held her breath. Eventually he shook his head. "I'm sorry. There's nothing else I can say." He took a step back, and the footman closed the door, locking it once again.

Jane sighed and thanked him before continuing toward her own bedroom. With the dance underway downstairs and footmen attending the guests, she'd completed her duties for the evening.

Reaching her room, she entered and closed the door behind her. An early night would be welcome if she could manage it and would give her a chance to think. She needed to go back over everything she knew and see if she'd missed some small detail along the way.

A crack of thunder in the distance brought her attention to the window, and she crossed the floor to look out. It was dark though, too dark to see if rain threatened.

Her heart lurched in her chest. Perhaps this was it, the night when she'd have the chance to return. Except if she did, it would be without James. So how could she? Leaving him here and building a life without him no longer seemed possible. And yet, to remain here…

She pushed her concerns aside and ran her fingers absently over the lacquered window sill. It wobbled slightly beneath her touch, as if an imperfection prevented it from lying completely flat. Instinctively, Jane pushed down a little bit firmer and watched as it happened again. Clearly the wood had come loose and was merely balancing in place.

An odd idea crossed her mind. Surely not. And yet, she'd always dreamed of finding a hidden compartment and weren't old houses renowned for such things? Determined to find out, she lifted the sill and set it aside, revealing a space in the wall.

Excitement filled her as she leaned forward to peer inside, unsure of what exactly she might be about to find, if anything at all. And then her heart shuddered as a small, leather-bound book came into view. Jane reached inside and pulled it out, turning it over in her hands before opening it with trembling fingers. A neat script greeted her on the first page, stating simply that this was the property of Betsy Andrews.

Jane crossed to her bed and sank down onto the

mattress, then flipped the page and started to read while pure exhilaration flooded her veins. Because this was no simple book. It was Betsy's diary. And if the maid had known something about her mistress – a detail that might have led to her death – perhaps she'd written about it somewhere here for Jane to find.

CHAPTER FOURTEEN

"HAVE YOU TOLD YOUR MOTHER you and I have no intention of forming an attachment?" James asked Lady Elise while taking a tour of the ballroom with her. It was the least he could do to appease his mother and also ensured she would leave him alone for a while.

"Not yet. She is very eager to unite our families." Lady Elise chuckled. "Telling her there is no hope of such a thing happening will be...difficult."

"You think it might be easier if you have another eligible suitor vying for your hand?"

A spark of mischief lit her eyes. "Why Camden! How well you know me already."

He laughed, earning looks of approval from not only his mother, but from Rockwell and Lady Rockwell too. "I fear your brother might be disappointed as well. He and I have been friends so long, I believe he hoped we could be more."

"Yes, well, he will simply have to get over it." She placed her hand over his and leaned slightly closer. "I realize Harrington intended to marry your sister and is still mourning her loss, but perhaps—"

"I would advise against it," James told her

abruptly. Noting her stunned surprise, he hastened to say, "What he feels goes much deeper than he is willing to show in public. It could be years before he recovers from his loss and longer still before he is ready to consider courting another woman."

"How tragic," Lady Elise murmured. "Your sister was lucky to have known such love."

James bit his tongue and merely nodded while guiding Lady Elise toward the refreshment table. Another glass of champagne was clearly in order, and once he had it in hand, he downed it swiftly before reaching for another.

"I plan on getting some fresh air," Rockwell said as he sidled up next to his sister. "Care to join me, Camden?"

"If Lady Elise can spare me," James said. A brief escape from the ballroom would be most welcome.

Lady Elise smiled. "I need to visit the retiring room anyway," she said, "so by all means, please go ahead."

Promising to dance with her when he returned, James followed Rockwell through the French doors and out into the cool evening air. He glanced up, expecting to see the sky filled with stars. Instead, grey clouds obscured his view. They hung in clumps, promising a heavy downpour later, and all he could think of was Jane. He ought to let her know, just in case.

"A cigar?" Rockwell held one toward him.

"No thank you." He watched Rockwell clip his and light it. "I am sorry your stay here could not have been better."

Rockwell choked on a deep inhale and smoke sputtered out of his mouth as he coughed. "Seriously, Camden. Your sister died and you feel the need to apologize?" He shook his head. "I only wish I could have done more to help you through it. Are you any closer to discovering who did it?"

Deciding not to reveal anything until he was certain, James shook his head. "No. I fear the case may go unsolved." He puffed out a breath and sipped his champagne. "If only the bloody magistrate had not been away on business."

"Each district ought to have several, for situations such as these."

"I agree."

A bit of silence settled between them before Rockwell said, "I hope you and my sister can form an attachment. There is no one I would rather welcome into the family than you, Camden. You are an excellent friend. The best, in fact, which is why I regret having to leave here in another couple of days." He drew on his cigar and puffed out a silky plume of smoke. "Business calls, however. I cannot put it off any longer."

"A title does not come without great responsibility. I understand you completely, Rockwell, and am simply grateful for the time you were able to spare."

He nodded. "Perhaps you and your mother will come to visit me in the autumn? We could even spend Christmas together, if you like."

"I will let you know," James said, hoping he wouldn't be bringing just his mother but Jane as well, if he chose to accept the invitation.

A drop of water fell on his hand and another dotted his forehead. "I believe it's starting to rain." A tiny flash of light illuminated the sky, followed by a clap of thunder. "If you will excuse me." He had to tell Jane that this might be her chance to leave, perhaps her only chance ever, and as much as he hoped she would stay, he didn't want her to have regrets.

But as he turned with the intention of going to fetch her, he found her standing but a few feet away with a book clutched between her hands. She glanced swiftly at Rockwell, acknowledging his presence before locking her gaze with James's.

"We were wrong," she said as she stepped toward him. "Completely and utterly wrong. From the very beginning."

"What do you mean?" Another drop fell on his cheek.

She stared at him, seemingly heedless of the wind picking up around them and of the clouds threatening to split open over their heads. "We made an assumption, James."

"James?" Rockwell voiced his surprise over Jane's use of his given name.

"What assumption?" James asked, ignoring his friend who would only tease him about his lack of control where his maid was concerned. The man would laugh if James told him he'd fallen in love with her.

"That your sister was killed first." Jane took a step forward. She looked at him as if he was all that mattered, as if no one else existed, and it was only the two of them here on the terrace about to be drenched in a downpour. "We believed Betsy was killed because she witnessed the crime and had to be silenced, because we found her second rather than first. But what if...what if that wasn't the case? What if it was the other way around?"

James stared back at Jane as more droplets fell, splattering against them with increasing frequency. "Then we were looking for motive in all the wrong places, considering all the wrong suspects."

"Exactly." A flash of lightning zigzagged across the sky, and a deafening boom followed as rain spilled over their heads.

"I'm going inside," Rockwell said, "before I get any wetter."

As if awoken by his voice, Jane pointed at Rockwell. "You did it," she said, halting him in his tracks.

"What are you talking about?" he asked as he turned toward her with a flicker of anger in his eyes. "How dare you make accusations without any proof?"

"I have this," Jane said as she wrapped her arms tight around the book to protect it from getting wet. Water streaked over her face, plastering her hair to her forehead and making her clothes cling tightly to her body. "It's Betsy's diary, and it's all the proof we need."

"What do you mean?" James asked.

"Camden," Rockwell grit between clenched teeth. "You cannot seriously be considering listening to what this woman has to say?"

"Stay where you are," James warned his friend before repeating his question to Jane. "What do you mean?"

"I mean Betsy and Rockwell were involved." She gave James a look that said it all. "More than that, Betsy realized she was pregnant by him and wrote of her intention to confront him about it and—"

"The girl was obsessed, Camden," Rockwell

insisted. "What she wrote about me in her diary has no bearing on reality because it is nothing but fiction."

"Apparently, she wanted him to help support and care for the child," Jane continued, "noting that she intended to go to her mistress for help if he refused to do so."

"Is this true?" James asked. "Or is this made up as well?"

Rockwell glared, his body outlined in an eerie relief as another bolt of lightning flashed in the sky. "Betsy chased after me from dawn until dusk from the moment I got here. If that got her pregnant, then this is the first I am hearing of it."

"So you deny it?" James asked, hoping to God what he feared wasn't true and that the man who'd been his friend since childhood was not responsible for killing two women just to avoid facing the repercussions.

"Of course I do," Rockwell yelled. He waved a hand in Jane's direction. "And the fact you would even consider believing such rubbish from her instead of trusting me is galling! Just goes to show the power she wields over you, a mere maid controlling an earl. It's disgusting!"

"And yet," Jane said, her voice carrying with unencumbered clarity, "I know you bedded her. To suppose she got with child—"

"Is possible. Yes. But to assume it was mine is a stretch."

James's jaw dropped. "So you did bed her then and discuss her being pregnant?"

Rockwell's shoulders tensed. "She wanted money which I was hardly about to give her."

"But it was more than that. Was it not?" A chill swept over James, and it wasn't because of the rain. "She threatened to tell Tatiana who would likely have come to me for advice. Worse, there was the chance Tatiana wasn't the only person Betsy would mention this to. Word gets around, gossip spreads, and the scandal of it all could have ruined your entire family's reputation."

"Many men survive having by-blows," Rockwell said.

"Yes," James agreed. "*After* they are married and the incident poses no risk to their prospects." He stared back at Rockwell through the sheet of falling rain. Fists clenched at either side and his evening clothes soaked all the way to his skin, he willed himself to ask the necessary question. "Did you kill Betsy and Tatiana?"

Rockwell heaved a large breath and expelled it, his eyes locked with James's.

"Did you?" James repeated.

Another pause followed while rain drummed against the large granite slabs beneath their feet. "I never meant to hurt Tatiana," he eventually said, "but she must have seen me carrying Betsy out to the stables, because she followed me there. And then when she realized what I had done, she ran."

"And then what?" James asked while nausea pushed at his throat. As difficult as it was, he needed to know what had happened that evening. He owed it to his sister.

"I chased her, but couldn't quite catch her until she arrived on the terrace. Everything after that was messy, unplanned. I feared she'd bring attention so I knew I had to act quickly." Softening his voice, he quietly said, "I reached for my knife, silencing her with one swift stroke." The words barely left his lips before James launched himself at him, hands slipping through water as he took the earl down in a tangle of limbs.

James pulled his arm back, adding momentum as he thrust his fist squarely into Rockwell's face. "Murderous bastard!" He punched him again while Rockwell pushed at his shoulder with one hand and tried to shove him aside with the other.

They rolled sideways and James's elbow struck the ground with a thwack. "Aaargh!" He grit his teeth, the pain preventing him from avoiding the punch he received seconds later. It cracked his nose, producing a warm trickle against his cheek as his blood mingled with the rain. "I'll see you hang for this!"

"The devil you will," Rockwell spat. His arm pulled back, and James prepared for another punch to the face. Instead, he caught a flicker of something shiny and silver and instinctively reached up to push his thumb straight into Rockwell's left eye.

The blade he'd only glimpsed for a second slashed past his face, so close it made the air hum in response to the movement.

"No!"

Jane's scream rang in James's ears as he shifted sideways, struggling to grab hold of Rockwell's wrist before he tried to stab him again. Finding purchase, he latched on hard to the other earl's arm and shoved him back. But Rockwell's position gave him the advantage, and he quickly regained his balance, coming at James again while rain splashed all around them and lightning brightened the sky overhead.

Gaining some space James pulled back his arm and punched Rockwell again, making him falter. The blade missed its mark, disappearing once more from James's line of view. Pushing back, James rolled Rockwell onto his back, dominating the fight at the same exact moment the world cracked open.

James stared, unable to tear his gaze from the distorted scenery or from Jane who stood so close, it would take but a couple of steps for her to vanish through the tear that linked their worlds for a moment. "Go," he yelled, knowing he probably wouldn't make it in time to join her. Not with Rockwell still clinging to him. And not when he had to make sure Tatiana's murderer got the punishment he deserved. "I love you, Jane. I always will. Now go!"

But to his dismay she screamed and charged toward him with anger and fear carved into her face. "Wha—"

She fell on him and on Rockwell, her arms winding their way around James as she tumbled down over him, pushing him fiercely aside. The air was wrenched from his lungs as he fell back against the wet terrace. It took a moment to adjust to what had happened and once he did, dread assailed him like a serpent wrapping itself around his body and crushing his chest.

"Jane!" Her much smaller body fought against Rockwell. With both hands she gripped his arm to ward off the blade while he made a grab for her throat and squeezed.

Her eyes bulged and James's heart exploded. It

was as if time slowed to a crawl while he pushed himself from the ground, praying to reach her in time as the horror played out before him. Jane loosened her hold on the arm that would thrust the blade forward and instinctively clasped Rockwell's hand in an effort to pry his fingers away from her throat. But he was larger, more powerful, and his eyes blazed with murderous intent.

"Rockwell!" James shot to his feet and sprang forward while forcing momentum into the fist he directed toward Rockwell's head.

The blade rose and descended toward Jane's chest, disappearing from view as Jane lurched to one side, just as James's fist crashed against Rockwell's skull. The thud reverberated up his arm in a dull and bone-deep ache, the sound of his knuckles crunching drowning out Rockwell's grunt and Jane's strangled scream.

Footsteps clicked and voices shouted, and James vaguely sensed Harrington's and Thompson's presence. But whatever they were saying was lost to him as he struggled to hear proof of life from Jane who'd collapsed on top of her assailant.

"Jane." He pulled her into his arms while someone else dragged Rockwell away from her.

James pressed his lips to her cheek and prayed. And still he listened while he murmured her name again and again and again. Until he heard it, the tiniest whisper of breath, confirming she lived. Christ! Tears welled in his eyes as he pulled her closer, not caring about the rain or the cold but simply needing to hold her.

"He stabbed you." It was all he could say without choking.

She coughed and inhaled with a shuddering wheeze. "No." She shifted a little and groaned. "It's just a scratch." She coughed again. "His grip on my throat almost ended me though. I'm glad you overpowered him when you did, or we probably wouldn't be talking right now."

He expelled a shuddering breath. To think how easily he could have lost her made his lungs constrict against the tightening of his chest. "You missed your chance though, Jane." Relief and regret warred inside him as he acknowledged the magnitude of her choice. "You could have gone home."

"No," she murmured, so faintly he could barely hear her. "Rockwell was going to kill you, and since I couldn't let that happen, I chose the future I want for myself. The one that includes you."

Speechless, he pressed a kiss to her brow and inhaled her fragrance. It was stronger now, accentuated by the rain. "We should get you inside before you catch a chill. Influenza can be especially unpleasant."

"I honestly don't know how you manage without a pharmacy nearby."

"A pharmacy?"

"I'm sure I'll figure it out though," she added as he stood and gathered her up in his arms. He wasn't really sure what she was talking about, so he paid extra attention while carrying her past his mother and Lady Rockwell who both looked as though they'd just seen him walk out of hell. Which he supposed they had, in a way.

"Not now," he said when his mother opened her mouth. He marched right past her while Lady Elise hurried along beside him to help with opening doors. "Please tell Margaret and a couple of footmen to ready a bath," he said when they arrived upstairs. "We need to get her out of these clothes as quickly as possible."

Without questioning him, Lady Elise disappeared from the room. It was the same one Jane had been allocated the night she'd arrived and in James's opinion it suited her far better than Betsy's smaller and more modest chamber ever had.

Setting her carefully on her feet, James ignored his own discomfort as he quickly undid the ties on Jane's dress and pulled it off over her head. Her teeth chattered and her body shook with violent shivers. Blood smeared the area between her shoulder and breast where she'd been wounded, staining the left side of her chemise in red.

Anger rose inside James again as he thought of what might have happened if she hadn't moved as fast as she had. For her sake, he tamped down the harsh emotions and started undoing her stays. When she flinched in response to his touch, he calmed his movements, doing his best to avoid her cut.

"Please hurry," she said, her voice tripping over her trembling lips.

He reached for the hem of her chemise and drew the garment off swiftly, then reached for the blanket covering the bedspread and pulled it around her shoulders, wrapping her in the warmth of the wool and concealing her nudity seconds before the footmen and Margaret arrived.

"Here," James said after lighting a fire in the grate. He guided her toward it. "Stay here until your bath is ready. I will return in a moment."

She fumbled clumsily with the blanket until she found a gap through which she was able to extend her hand. Her fingers touched his, and he felt his heart stutter while heat seeped under his skin. "Thank you."

He stepped toward her and kissed her lips, heedless of who might happen to see. "It is I who should be thanking you," he said. Reaching up he brushed a wet lock of hair from her forehead. "You sacrificed everything for me this evening and saved my life in the process. Whatever it takes, no matter what I must do, I will ensure your happiness, Jane. You can count on that."

Reluctantly, he quit her room and hurried on over to his. Discarding his jacket and vest, he peeled off his soggy shirt, and stepped out of his trousers and smalls. Socks followed in quick succession until he was utterly naked. Crossing to his wardrobe, he grabbed a towel and wiped himself down, removing as much of the clamminess as possible before locating fresh clothes and getting dressed once again. His own bath would have to wait. He'd warm himself by the fire in Jane's room for now. But leaving her alone any longer was not an option. She called to him, the need to be with her and to know she was safe demanding he hurry back to her room as quickly as possible.

When he returned, the footmen were just leaving while Margaret stood next to the bath ready to assist.

"You may go," James told her.

Margaret glanced at Jane, then back at James. "Are you certain?"

He gave her a decisive nod. "Yes." When she still hesitated, he said, "You need not worry, Margaret. My intentions are perfectly honorable. I mean to marry Jane as soon as possible."

The astonishment on Margaret's face was undeniable. Her lips parted and her eyes widened. "Oh," was all she managed to say, and, "Well then." She crossed the floor, pausing briefly beside Jane to give her a quick hug before bobbing a curtsey on her way out the door. It closed firmly behind her, leaving James and Jane quite alone in the room.

"Come on," James said as he put his arm around Jane's shoulders and urged her toward the bath. With the most delicate touch he could manage, he removed the blanket she wore and helped her into the steaming hot water.

Her sigh of pleasure and the perfect view she gave him of her elegant back and gorgeous bottom sent a dart of desire straight to his groin. He sucked in a breath and expelled it slowly while forcing himself to consider her needs. She was wounded, after all, and in need of comfort, not lust.

With this in mind, he handed her the soap. "Can you manage on your own?" he asked.

She nodded, allowing him to retreat to the spot in front of the fire. "I still find it hard to believe Rockwell killed both Betsy and my sister," he said after a while. The sound of water lapping about soothed his senses while the warmth from the flames pushed aside any lingering cold.

"He panicked," Jane said.

"But he was like family." The idea of it and the lack of morality needed for someone to act so callously was shocking. The fact Rockwell knew them, had danced with Tatiana last season and laughed with her during conversation, strolled with her and played cards with her, made it more unfathomable and worse.

"I know." Jane was watching him with regret in her eyes. "I'm sorry it turned out to be him, James."

"Me too." He averted his gaze and stared into the flickering flames before him while Jane climbed out of the bath. "His sister's prospects are ruined."

"Oh my God! I didn't even think of that." Jane picked up a towel and wound it around her slender figure. "Poor girl."

Casting a look in her direction and seeing blood begin to pebble once more around her wound, James found a clean handkerchief and went to press it against her. "Can you hold this in place for a minute?" When she nodded, he went to fetch a bottle of brandy from his room, along with one of the rolled linen strips he kept for this exact purpose.

"This is bound to sting a bit," he told Jane as he grabbed another clean handkerchief, dampened it with a splash of the brandy, and held it up for her to see. When she nodded, he removed the previous one he'd given her and pressed the newly prepared one over the wound.

She hissed on a sharp inhale, her entire body going immediately tense.

"Sorry," he murmured.

"It's all right. The last thing I need is an infection."

"I quite agree." He began unwinding the strip of linen, using it to tie the handkerchief securely in place. "Which is why we need to keep an eye on this and change the compress regularly." Locating her nightgown, he helped her into it with as much indifference as he could muster. Which wasn't a lot.

"Will you stay with me tonight?" she asked once he'd finished.

He nodded. "Of course. Leaving you now after everything you have been through is out of the question." Considering the still warm bath water, he contemplated a quick soak but then decided against it. He was tired and so was she, judging from her red-rimmed eyes and the yawn she kept trying to hold down.

So he pulled the counterpane back and waited for her to climb into bed before joining her on the other side. Still fully clothed to avoid the sort of contact that would invariably lead to arousal, he hooked his arm over her side so her back was pressed snugly against his chest.

"I love you, James." She whispered the words as her breathing settled into a slumberous rhythm.

He inhaled the fragrant scent of honey still clinging to her hair while his heart latched onto those words. "I love you too, Jane. I always will."

CHAPTER FIFTEEN

FOUR WEEKS HAD PASSED SINCE Rockwell's arrest. He'd since been found guilty on two counts of murder, stripped of his title, and sentenced to death by hanging. From what Jane had heard, a silk rope had been commissioned in deference to his rank though she and James did not yet know when the execution was scheduled to take place.

Trying not to think of it since she did not want her mood to be dimmed on this particular day, Jane smoothed her hands over her skirts and regarded herself in the mirror. A smile touched her lips in response to the vision that greeted her. Expensive baby-blue silk fell in soft folds around her, trimmed with the finest white lace. Beneath her breasts was a wide satin sash, tied neatly in a voluminous bow at her back.

It was quite a departure from the grey servant attire she'd worn for the first week she'd been here. But all of that had changed the moment James announced their engagement. Which he'd done the morning after she'd told him she loved him. The happy news had seemed to brighten the atmosphere a little, even if James's mother had looked as though she'd just been informed of her son's death as well.

Jane sighed. Hopefully the dowager countess would come to accept her eventually. Until then, Jane chose to smile and focus on the happiness flowing through her. This was her wedding day after all, the most unexpectedly wonderful experience of her life.

"Are you ready?"

Jane turned toward Elise who stood in the doorway.

"She will be in a second," Margaret said as she picked up a diamond necklace and hung it around Jane's neck. "There. As pretty as a princess."

"Camden won't know what hit him," Elise said, her eyes twinkling as Jane came toward her.

She grinned. "Thank you for coming."

"Thank you for inviting me." Elise met Jane's gaze with a frankness Jane wouldn't have expected from someone so young. "Most of our friends have cut us off. The stigma is one we will never escape and our lack of title and the land that went with it has significantly diminished our status, which means Mama is now quite determined to see me marry above my rank."

Jane sympathized. "Perhaps you'll meet someone here during the wedding."

Elise managed a smile. "You forget that only the most desperate of peers would think to consider me now."

"Then forget what your mother wants and make your own choice the way James and I did. Marry for love, Elise, and I have no doubt you'll be happy."

"I'll certainly consider it," Elise said as she took Jane's arm and guided her out into the hallway. They proceeded to the stairs and descended toward the foyer where the servants awaited.

Jane looked at them all in turn, at Mrs. Fontaine and at Cook, at Tilly who stood beside Mr. Goodard, and Hendricks whose serious expression slipped a notch the moment their eyes met. Mr. Snypes, of course, had been fired on account of inappropriate behavior and disloyalty, his position now filled by a Mr. Finch.

Passing them all, Jane swept out of the house and into the awaiting carriage with Elise climbing in behind her.

"When I see you again, you'll be the Countess of Camden," Margaret said as she helped arrange Jane's skirts around her feet. She glanced up and smiled. "Good luck." The door closed and the conveyance rolled into motion, scattering Jane's nerves like a swarm of butterflies taking to the sky.

Excitement and trepidation whirled inside her, twisting her stomach until she felt slightly ill. This was it, the biggest decision she'd ever made, and as right as it felt and as much as she wanted to go through with it, she couldn't quite shake her concerns. After all, she wasn't the only one giving up everything for this marriage. James was too, his decision to marry his maid sending shockwaves through every level of society.

When the invitations had gone out, many had sent their regrets, and although he'd shrugged off the blatant disapproval of his peers, Jane couldn't help but wonder if it didn't bother him just a little, knowing he'd been shunned.

But when she stepped inside the church and saw him waiting by the altar with Harrington by his side and her eyes met his across the distance, she knew they had no choice but to wed. Because this was what love felt like, that invisible bond linking them together and easing her troubles with nothing but assurance. His smile said it all, conveying without the need for words how much she meant to him and how happy he was to have her in his life.

She felt the same, and as she walked toward him, the butterflies disappeared somewhere over the horizon, leaving nothing but calm and the strongest sense of rightness she'd ever felt in her life. This was what mattered. Them, together, forever, as one. He was her best friend, her confidant and her lover, and as he slipped the ring on her finger a short while later and bent his head to kiss her, she silently thanked the universe for its interference. As impossible as it seemed, she'd found the man she was destined to be with and nothing in the world felt better than that.

"Have I told you how stunning you look?" James asked as he came to stand beside her.

Needing a bit of fresh air, Jane had stepped out onto the terrace. Her hand rested on the balustrade as she gazed out over the sun-kissed garden before her. The weather was fine, perfect for a wedding, with birds chirping in the nearby foliage and heat warming her skin.

"About ten times or so," she said with a smile while accepting the glass of champagne he handed to her. "Have I told you how dashing you look?"

His lips hitched into something she easily recognized as the beginnings of a mischievous grin. "I believe so, but I will happily hear it again."

She laughed and playfully slapped his arm. "You are incorrigible."

"Incorrigibly in love with you," he murmured in that seductive tone that weakened her knees. His arm wound around her shoulder, pulling her closer to his side. "What prompted you to stay?"

They'd never really discussed it; there had been so much else to deal with in the wake of Rockwell's arrest and their ensuing wedding preparations. "I couldn't leave you." Her heart ached at the very thought of her choosing a different path – a path without him by her side. "Not just because Rockwell threatened your life and saving you mattered more to me in that moment than anything else, but because I need you, James. It wasn't really a choice in the end. It was the only way forward for me."

His lips brushed her forehead with slow and whisper-soft tenderness. "It would have destroyed me, I think, if you'd gone. I cannot even begin to imagine how—"

"Then don't." She turned in his arms, her eyes burning with pent-up emotion. "I am here, James, and I have no intention of going anywhere. This is where I will build my life. Here, with you."

As she said it, she reflected on how she'd changed the course of history. When she'd first arrived at Summervale as a tourist, records had shown that Tatiana's murder had remained unsolved and that James had never married. All of that would be different now and Jane could only hope that the universe's plan for her to meet James had not offset its balance.

Affection warmed James's gaze as he drew her more firmly against him. And then his lips found hers, desperate for assurance and eager for their celebration to be over, so they could retreat upstairs and enjoy the rest of their day alone. "You mean the world to me, Jane," he said between kisses. "You are my compass, my certainty, my heart."

"As you are mine," she promised, meaning it with every fiber of her being. "You are my destiny, my future, my love."

ACKNOWLEDGMENTS

I WOULD LIKE TO THANK THE Killion Group for their incredible help with the editing and formatting of this book. My thanks also go to Chris Cocozza for providing the stunning artwork. And to my wonderful beta-readers, Maria Rose, Susan Down Lucas and Jacqueline Ang, thank you for your insight and advice. You made this story shine!

ABOUT THE AUTHOR

BORN IN DENMARK, SOPHIE HAS spent her youth traveling with her parents to wonderful places around the world. She's lived in five different countries, on three different continents, has studied design in Paris and New York, and has a bachelor's degree from Parson's School of Design. But most impressive of all – she's been married to the same man three times, in three different countries, and in three different dresses.

While living in Africa, Sophie turned to her life-long passion – writing.

When she's not busy dreaming up her next romance novel, Sophie enjoys spending time with her family. She currently lives on the East Coast.

You can contact her through her website at *www.sophiebarnes.com*

Follow her on Amazon and Bookbub to receive new release updates for her books.

And please consider leaving a review for this book.

Every review is greatly appreciated!

Made in the USA
Coppell, TX
04 December 2020

42937086R00152